TALES OF THE IRISH ROSE

TALES OF THE IRISH ROSE
by Mark Hilgers and Jerry D. Young
Published by Creative Texts Publishers
PO Box 50
Barto, PA 19504
www.creativetexts.com

The following is a work of fiction. Any resemblance to actual names, persons, businesses, and incidents is strictly coincidental. Locations are used only in the general sense and do not represent the real place in actuality.

ISBN: 978-0-578-52564-8

TALES OF THE IRISH ROSE

by

MARK HILGERS AND JERRY D. YOUNG

CREATIVE TEXTS PUBLISHERS
Barto, Pennsylvania

TABLE OF CONTENTS

CHAPTER ONE

Present Day, outside Philadelphia, Pennsylvania

Lee and Cord thought they were finished cleaning out Uncle Phil's house. It had already taken two weeks to complete all the arrangements and other tasks necessary after a family member dies.

With Uncle Phil being the pack rat he was in general, and inclined to keep every scrap of paper, book, magazine article, newspaper article, and any other media he found with information about his specialty, the removal of all of his accumulation was taking a great deal of additional time.

Uncle Phil was a historian, with his main work and interest being Pennsylvanian sports teams. Having taught at the college level all his adult life, he had literally tons of material.

Most of it was going to various colleges and museums, and some to libraries. The rest would simply be stored with everything else that did not have another home.

Out of respect for their uncle, neither Lee nor Cord were inclined to destroy any of it. Since their family business had three large warehouses, one with climate-controlled areas, those things would be taken there and stored. "Until such time as we can actually do something else with it," Lee told Cord when they loaded the last of the boxes in the hired truck that would take the material to Florida.

"Better take one last walk through," Cord said, as the truck drove away. He wiped his forehead. It was a hot and humid day here in the rural area outside Philadelphia.

"Probably right," Lee replied, taking a long drink from her water bottle. "Never know what Uncle Phil might have put somewhere and forgot about."

They went in the front door and turned right. The big, rambling old house had many rooms, some connected directly together, others opening off hallways. It took a full hour to go through each room, open each door in each room, and check what was behind it.

They had been careful and thorough during the cleanup, so did not find anything they had missed. Until they got to Uncle Phil's bedroom, the last room on the walk through. A quick look around the empty room, and the last thing to check was the closet. Both remembered emptying it out, but they did not cut corners for anything, because in their line of work, cutting corners could cost a life.

Cord opened the closet door of the walk-in closet, and Lee stepped inside. The house had been updated several times since it was built in the late 1700s, and Uncle Phil's bedroom suite had been the latest one, incorporating an en suite bath and the large walk-in closet.

Lee did a slow turn, looking at the bare walls, clothes hanging racks and bars, and the many cubbyholes for Uncle Phil's infamous sweater collection. Just to be sure, Lee opened the cabinets that had held odds and ends. As she was closing the last one, something caught her eye and she paused, staring, the door held half open.

"Lee?" Cord asked when he saw her squat down and look closer.

"Cord, come look at this," Lee said, moving over so Cord could squat down beside her. "Did you notice this before?"

It took a moment for Cord to see what Lee was pointing toward. "No. I didn't," he said. Standing, Cord went to the end of the base cabinets and looked at the wall. "I do not believe this," he said, reaching out to touch a switch on the wall.

Some lights that would illuminate whatever was hanging on the closet pole below them came on. A few seconds later, a wall panel slowly swung open toward him. If anything had been hanging on the rod, it would have prevented the door from opening, Cord decided when he touched the door and felt no resistance. The secret door was not power operated. The switch only released a solenoid that unlocked it so it could open.

"Holy Moley!" exclaimed Lee, standing beside Cord, looking into the hidden room. "Uncle Phil had some secrets, I take it."

"It sure looks like it," Cord said, ducking under the closet pole and entering the room. Lee was right behind him.

It did not take long for the two to decide that Uncle Phil's secrets were not all that remarkable. There were a few high-quality totes on some shelves, each containing, after they opened them, family records and documents going back many years. Pictures, documents, and all the other things a family is prone to gather and keep. It was the same in each tote.

"He has family records from every branch of the family," Lee said.

Cord paused. "You know," he said, looking thoughtful, "I seem to remember Pop saying that Uncle Phil was sort of the family historian. That whenever someone would die, the other members of the family would gather up their stuff and take it to Uncle Phil. I guess... Kind of like what we are doing with his stuff."

"You must be right," Lee replied, opening another tote to find yet another family ancestor's family papers.

Cord had to move a tote down from an upper shelf for Lee, so she could check it while he did another. As each was given a cursory look, they would take it out to the bedroom. When all the totes were inspected and moved, Cord took a last look around, ready to leave. Lee was taking another long drink of water, emptying her bottle. With her head tilted back, her eyes went to the top shelf.

She sputtered water, some of it hitting Cord. "Hey!" he exclaimed.

Trying to clear her throat, Lee could only point to the shelf.

"What?" Cord asked. "I took the last tote..." Cord's words faded away and he took a step back to stand beside his sister. "I guess I didn't," he muttered, moving toward the shelves again.

He reached up and back, feeling around. Finding a folding handle, Cord grasped it and pulled. The large, heavy fire-resistant storage container nearly hit him in the face when it came off the shelf, much heavier than he expected.

He set it down, and this time, very carefully, stepped onto the lowest shelf and stood up. Now he could see the full span of the top shelves that ran around three of the walls. He spotted one more of the fire-resistant containers, a bit further down the same shelf. He grabbed it and stepped down, letting the heavy container swing clear of the shelves, Lee, and himself. If anything, this one was even heavier.

Cord and Lee looked at the two containers, both essentially very large fire safes, and then each other. "Keys?" Lee asked after a moment.

"Hm..." Cord muttered. "They could not possibly..." He reached into his left pants pocket and pulled out Uncle Phil's key ring. It was a large ring, with many keys. After several tries, Cord had both fire-resistant containers unlocked.

Brother and sister shared another look, and then each opened one of the containers.

Lee spoke first. Or, rather, whistled, and then said, "Crimeny!"

This time it was Cord that muttered "Holy Moley!"

Handling it carefully, Lee removed something wrapped in fine leather. She had to set it down on one of the shelves so she could unwrap whatever it was. When she did, Cord and Lee stared at the old leather-bound book. When Lee went to open it, she found that the covers were wood with the leather covering them.

It was in remarkably good shape, considering the date written on the first page. She gasped then. "This is her journal!"

"Whose journal?" asked Cord.

"Aislinn's"

"Aislinn's? As in the original Aislinn? The one from Ireland?"

Lee could only nod. She carefully turned several more pages. "This is amazing..."

Cord looked over her shoulder for a moment. Lee closed the journal, moved it aside and picked up the even larger book below it in the bundle. It too was a journal. As was each of the other two items that had been wrapped in the leather.

Lee looked over at the container. Rather tentatively she picked up another leather wrapped item. This one was a bible. A large, ornate, engraved and illustrated bible. Next, Lee took out a beautiful wooden box from the safe. When she opened it, she found a complete lady's correspondence tool set. Ink bottles, dip pens, blotters, jars of sand, several quills, and a set of quill tools.

Another large, beautiful wooden box opened to reveal exquisite period woman's jewelry.

The last item she removed was heavy. Heavy enough that she grunted slightly when she picked it up. It was a leather bag, closed with a leather drawstring. Not realizing she was holding her breath; Lee worked the bag open. She gasped again, drawing needed air into her lungs. She held the bag so Cord could look inside.

"Gold coins..." was all he said. He turned to the other fire-resistant container. The largest one. Lee set the leather bag of gold coins back into the first safe, and moved over beside Cord.

He went through the same process, finding much the same sort of things as Lee had found in the first container. Besides journals, however, were a set of similarly bound ship's logbooks. There was a correspondence kit, a smaller jewelry box, and three, rather than one leather bag. One was pretty much identical to the first one. Gold coins.

The other two, however, were much different. Smaller, for one thing. And with clasps rather than leather drawstrings. The main thing was the contents of the two bags. One was filled almost to the point the clasp would not close with a variety of gems, pearls, and other similar items. "Hm," Cord muttered, "not a single ruby or emerald..."

Then came an "Oh..." when he opened the other bag, stuffed just as full. With rubies and emeralds.

Brother and sister exchanged another look, both with lifted eyebrows. And then they both looked over at the last item they had not yet checked. A rather simple looking upright cabinet. Rather like one that was in the kitchen pantry that had held cleaning supplies.

Cord opened the double doors. The cabinet had two full-width upper shelves. Below them in the cabinet were two vertical pieces, dividing the area into three sections. Both shelves held several plain to fancy wooden cases. The lower sections held several longer wooden cases, and even more in number of long, hard leather cases.

Reverently now, the two began to check the contents. And found weapons of several kinds from the same period as what was in the fire-resistant containers. There were also many accoutrements for the weapons.

In silence, everything was moved to the bedroom. Then, Cord and Lee did one more, very thorough, inspection of the hidden room. And were actually relieved that they found nothing else.

It took a while longer for the two, still working silently, to load everything they had found during the final walk through into Cord's Dodge pickup and Lee's Chevy Suburban.

Locking the house up carefully before they left, the stunned pair headed for their home on Georgia's Atlantic coastline.

For three months Lee and Cord sorted and read the documents Uncle Phil had stored away. They would take a few with them each time they went out on a job, and read during down time. When home, however, it became a full day job, other than a bit of necessary work to keep their small fleet ready to go at a moment's notice.

Their employees, both the shore-based ones, and the ships' crews, were excellent. The Lynches paid well, and provided a great benefits package. They needed and expected quality work, and they hired those that could provide that quality work.

Part of the reason they were able to keep good people was not just the pay and benefits. Lee and Cord were hands on bosses. They did not manage their employees. They led them. Both could, and did, every task that was required to accomplish the job at hand.

From swabbing decks to the difficult and dangerous hard suit diving in deep, cold, waters with erratic sea currents and often sharks and other dangerous creatures of the sea. The crews knew that they would be right there with them, not only helping, but making sure everyone worked safely, and that whoever they were working for did not try to cut any corners.

The last job they had just finished had been a tough one. It was one of the hard suit deep dives, to recover what they could of a work boat that had gone down between the Gulf coast and the off-shore oil rig it was servicing.

The primary goal was recovering any bodies that might still be on the ship and finding the logbook. Secondary would be evaluating and documenting the damage to the ship, to help determine why the ship went down.

It went well, technically. They were able to discover what happened, recovered the log book, and even quite a few of the crew's belongings and some important company documents and other articles.

And they were able to recover every one of the crew. Which was remarkable, and in terms of accomplishing the goal, satisfying. It was also heartbreaking.

It was obvious all of the crew had tried desperately to save the ship and themselves. From the looks of it, they had all faced the dangers bravely. And had failed to save the ship and themselves, through no fault of their own.

The worst of it was that, though the bodies were preserved fairly well by the cold water at that depth, it was only parts of them, for something, or several somethings had fed on them.

Cord was driving his truck from the docks to the Lynch Family Ocean Services offices, Lee riding beside him. She was quiet, looking out the window silently.

"You okay, Sis?" Cord asked, glancing over at her again.

She turned to face him, a wan look on her face. "Yeah. I guess. But that was difficult... I had no idea that one of the crew was Jeanette Wilson's brother."

"Oh," Cord replied softly. Lee and Jeanette's daughter, Polly, had been friends in high school.

A few minutes later, as Cord was parking the truck, he said, "Lee, why don't you take a vacation. You haven't really taken any time off for a long time."

"Do the words kettle and black mean anything to you?" Lee asked, smiling a bit when she looked over at Cord.

His cheeks pinked slightly. "Well... Tell you what. If you will take a couple of weeks off, so will I. We do not have anything pending that Jackie can't handle just fine."

Lee straightened up in the seat slightly. "Really? You are right, you know. Jackie probably needs to handle things on her own, at least for a short stint. She is certainly capable. But does need a bit of experience handling things without one of us right there. I think it would help her build up her confidence."

Cord nodded and they both got out of the truck. As they walked toward the rear entrance of the office building Lee asked Cord, "Do you know where William is at the moment?"

Cord shook his head. "No. Last I heard he was up at Machu Pichu. Doing some research on something a couple of mountains over. Some discovery he was notified about. Why are you asking?"

"I just thought that it would be good if he was here while we were gone. Jackie likes him, and he could lend a hand if necessary, without being here as her boss."

Cord held the door for Lee, a thoughtful look on his face. "You're right," he said as they shed their jackets and hung them on a coat hook. "Too bad we can't get ahold of him. That would work well."

Lee turned into the woman's restroom as Cord headed for the reception area to check in. He stopped when he entered, his mouth agape. "She did it again..." he muttered as he closed his mouth and stepped forward.

"Hey there Cuz!" said William. "Jackie said you guys were on the way in." They hugged briefly and shook hands.

"How was Machu Pichu?" Cord asked.

"Good," replied William. "Found a ceremonial site that had never been disturbed. Got things started for the locals and headed on back. Thought I would stop in and say hello. Been awhile."

"It has," Cord replied.

There was a gasp behind them and both turned. Lee was staring at William; her mouth open the way Cord's had been shortly before. "William! You're here!"

William grinned, looked down at himself and said, "So it appears."

"Oh, you!" Lee said and hurried over for a hug and kiss on the cheek.

"You're looking good, Lee. Found that special someone yet?"

Lee turned red. "No. And don't rush me." It was an ongoing battle that both seemed to enjoy.

William laughed. They moved into the break room and sat down at one of the tables. "What are you two up to now?"

Cord and Lee exchanged a glance. They both looked back at William. It was Lee that spoke. "Actually, that kind of depends on you."

"Me?" William asked, obviously startled.

Cord nodded. He checked to make sure Jackie was not around. "We're thinking about taking a couple of weeks off. This last job was tough and emotionally draining."

Fortunately, William nodded and Cord did not have to talk about it. "Jackie is ready to run the place without us, but she lacks a bit of confidence.

"We were actually just thinking that if you were here, kind of a back-up, she would be able to do just fine, knowing that she was not totally on her own even without you being her actual boss."

"She really doesn't need anyone," William said. "I was talking to her earlier and she seemed more than capable. Had a handle on everything she was explaining."

"We know," Lee said. "It is just that she gets nervous and doubts herself when someone isn't around. She has always made the right decision, but worries about things until it is clear that it was the right decision."

William nodded, looking off in the distance thoughtfully. When he looked back at Lee and then Cord, he asked, "When was the last time you two took a break, anyway?"

"It has been a while," Cord admitted.

"Yeah... I'll be glad to hang for a while. Might check out a few things in this area. Do some hiking and exploring."

Lee smiled. "That would be great, William. Thank you."

"Ditto, Cuz," Cord added. "Thanks. We were both kind of reluctant to take off, but I have to admit, now that it is kind of a done deal, I am really looking forward to it."

With the opportunity available, Lee and Cord both quickly decided, with only a short, mostly non-verbal, discussion, to finish up the research on their pirate ancestors and their ship, Irish Rose.

CHAPTER TWO

Late Seventeenth Century, Province of Georgia

"Aislinn, you need to go with the house staff. It is going to be too dangerous for you when Teniente Chavez gets here."

"I am not leaving without you, Markus! We are in this together. This is my home, too!"

Markus sighed. He seldom won an argument with his young sister, not yet eighteen. The same fiery Irish blood flowed through her veins as did through his.

The bright red hair and flashing green eyes were just two signs of it, matching his own.

Except he had learned to control his temper. It had been a must, if he was to build his fortune here in the New World. And he had.

Markus' thoughts drifted to the time before he and Aislinn left Ireland. His father had made it very clear that Markus' older brother Connor would inherit everything and Markus would have to make it on his own. Aislinn would marry old O'Dougal to join the two families when she was of age, or else.

When the opportunity came for Markus to go to the New World he did not hesitate. With Aislinn as perceptive as she was, being fae, it was not long before she cornered him and made him admit what he was planning. And invited herself along.

Markus had not protested very much. He did not like any of the O'Dougals, particularly the head of the clan. And did love his sister. Her arranged marriage in just a few years was the only thing that had bothered him about his plan. It bothered him enough that he agreed to let her accompany him.

He wracked his brain to try to come up with a way to ease the way for her. Their father would never consent to the plan, much less assist. Markus was not all that surprised that his mother discovered their plans, for she, like her daughter, was fae. Even more so than Aislinn.

Whether it was her normal senses or in some other way, she knew, and the day before he and Aislinn were to sneak away and head for the harbor to board the ship that would take them to the New World, his mother had taken him aside after supper and slipped him three large and one smaller leather purses. Two clinked, but the other two made no noise.

When Markus went to open them, his mother stilled his hands. "Only this one, for your journey, my son," she said, indicating one of the larger leather purses that had clinked. "Hide them away well. Take care of your sister. And write when you can. I love you, son."

"I love you, Mother." After a brief but heartfelt hug, Markus slipped away, headed for Aislinn's bedroom.

A quiet knock had Aislinn opening the door just enough for Markus to slip inside. Markus saw Aislinn's tear streaked face, then a slight movement behind her in the dark room caught his eye.

His eyes widened and he cut them back to Aislinn quickly. "Aislinn!" he whispered urgently. But before he could continue, Aislinn spoke. It was not a whisper, but she did keep her voice down.

"Markus… She found out. She always knows when I am up to something." Aislinn's voice dropped significantly. "I am beginning to think she is fae. But she won't admit it."

More loudly again, Aislinn continued, "She will not take no for an answer! She insists she must go along to take care of me." Aislinn turned her head slightly and looked at her hand maiden, Morgana.

So did Markus. Even in the faint light from the moonlit window, Morgana's eyes were bright, but not from tears. From excitement and, not unexpectedly, determination. Markus sighed slightly. Morgana was tall and though not particularly full figured, she was extremely strong and capable.

Only four inches shorter than Markus' own six three, she towered over Aislinn, who was only five two. Aislinn usually had no trouble getting Morgana to do what she wanted, but Morgana was loyal unto death, and it was her sworn oath to protect and care for Aislinn, taken a few days after Aislinn's birth when Morgana was hired to help Markus' and Aislinn's mother after the difficult pregnancy and birth.

Markus opened his mouth to tell Morgana she could not go with them, but closed it without speaking at the look in Morgana's face. It would be useless. There was no need for Morgana to tell him that she would follow Aislinn at a distance if Markus refused to let her go. Markus knew it.

And to be honest with himself, which he always was, Markus felt a sense of relief, knowing he would not have to take care of some of the details that a girl still shy of fourteen years of age would need as she became older and became a young woman.

Aislinn had one arm around Markus' waist. She wiped away the tears from her face when Markus asked Morgana, "You are packed?"

"Of course, sir," was her quick, quiet reply. "Milady's things are ready, as well. I will have no trouble handling them."

Markus nodded. "Very well. Be ready in fifteen minutes, at the rear gate. I need a moment with your mistress."

It was Morgana that nodded this time. She slipped out the door, after first opening it slightly to look both ways down the hallway.

Markus took Aislinn's shoulders in his hands. "Are you sure about this, Aislinn? The journey…"

"Oh, Markus! I am! I am! I do not want to marry O'Dougal! I was scared, for a while, but with Morgana… I'm sorry. I didn't tell her. I don't know how…"

Markus shook his head. "It is of no matter. She has her ways. And you could be right about her being fae." Markus shook his head. "It will probably be easier on all of us with her along. Now. We had better be going…"

"Markus," Aislinn said, putting her hand on his forearm as he started to turn away. "Mother knows, too."

"I know, Aislinn. She spoke to me just now. Gave me some purses…"

Aislinn's eyes widened. "She gave me her ring and necklace. And her blessing."

Markus nodded. "I am not surprised. She loves us very much. It is going to be difficult for her, I am afraid."

"She is strong, Markus," Aislinn said. "She will be fine."

Markus nodded, unwilling to allow Aislinn to see his worry. As had Morgana, Markus checked the hallway before leading the way out of Aislinn's bedroom.

The trip turned out to be uneventful. Even the weather cooperated, staying calm the entire journey. And with the money that their mother had given Markus, in addition to what Markus had accumulated, he was able to hire transport from New England to the wilderness of what would some day be called the State of Georgia.

Markus, with Aislinn's full support and more than a little help, carved out a place in the Georgia wilderness in a short period of time. At first it was simply a working farm to provide for their needs and the workers they hired, with enough to sell to not only maintain what was left of their funds, but actually start adding to them.

And as the years went by, the farm grew into a much larger operation, becoming a farm and ranch, with cattle and swine, then horses. Eventually the Lynch Estate became known for producing some of the finest horse flesh in the New World.

Add with the ever-growing need for ship masts, timbers and lumber that the Estate was able to supply in abundance, Markus and Aislinn became wealthy, far beyond the value their mother had given them. They still had all of the gems that had been in the smaller of the purses and had replaced the gold they had used in the other three.

Each now treasured the two purses each kept with the few other things they had brought with them to remind them of their mother and Ireland.

Markus was considered the most eligible bachelor in the area, though he was not looking to get married. Aislinn had more suitors than she could deal with. She, too, was not really looking to get married. Actually, having Markus for a brother as an example, she was holding out, dreaming of finding a Knight In Shining Armor of her own to love.

While it seemed to most in the area that the Lynches had an easy life, the truth was they both worked hard, first to gain what they had, then to maintain it, and even increase it.

Aislinn was not an idle Southern lady. She not only worked with the prize horses, she spent considerable time learning about healing from anybody who had knowledge and helping those in need in the local community, especially women and children, since there was very little medical help available.

The other primary worry that Markus had that most others in the area did not consider a threat, was the Spanish presence in Florida. Though they had mostly left Georgia, they were still the dominant force in Florida.

Markus had dealt with the English for the most part, selling the ships' masts, timbers, lumber and preserved food to both private shipping companies and the English Navy. But Still, he continued to get requests from the Spanish in Florida for his goods.

Reluctantly, he decided on an exploratory sales trip. He would take a selection of goods, see what the market looked like, and make a decision whether or not to deal with the Spaniards. There was no doubt he could sell what he took, either to private individuals in Florida or the Spanish Navy.

Markus did not even try to argue when Aislinn told him she was going with him. He just shook his head and then nodded. Aislinn had proven herself to be nearly as capable as himself, and he wondered sometimes if Morgana might not just best him in a fight, especially as he probably would not be willing to fight a woman, and Morgana would be more than willing to use any tactic, fair or not, to win to protect Aislinn.

With Ricardo Estrada, Markus' estate manager and foreman, half a dozen hired bullwhackers men to handle the oxen pulling the cargo wagons, two horse wranglers, and Morgana, he and Aislinn set out for Florida.

It was late spring, after all the planting had been done, and having left Ricardo's brother Hernando in charge of the estate, Markus felt no need to rush the trip. They took things easyto lessen the strain on the animals. Some of the trip was through less than pleasant parts of Georgia and northern Florida. Three weeks after they left the estate, they were at their destination there.

Experienced travelers now, a comfortable camp was set up outside of St. Augustine that Friday and Saturday. With the animals corralled and the crew settled, Markus, Aislinn, and the ever-present Morgana headed into the city to attend Mass at the Mission.

Markus was astride his prize Barb stallion, Leprechaun while Aislinn was dressed elegantly, riding sidesaddle on her mare, Spirit, and Morgana, having long ago adapted to wearing breeches and riding astride was on one of the geldings brought for possible sale.

When they entered the edge of St. Augustine they were immediately noticed. All three looked around curiously as they rode down the street toward the mission. Morgana looked with a neutral look on her face, watching for anything that might endanger her charge. Aislinn, however, was smiling, enjoying the experience.

Markus smiled when looked upon, but, like Morgana, he was keeping a sharp eye out for possible trouble.

Luckily nothing untoward occurred, and they arrived at the mission without incident. Markus helped his sister dismount. With the three on the ground, a young boy took the reins of the horses when Markus gave him a couple of coins. "Your horses will be well cared for, sir."

"Thank you," Markus replied, taking Aislinn's arm and heading for the door to the mission with Morgana trailing along behind. Again, they were watched with curiosity. Just before they reached the door, a commotion behind them had them turning around to see what the disturbance was.

Morgana frowned openly. Markus kept his face impassive, but Aislinn looked on curiously as several Spanish soldiers approached the mission on foot. In the lead was a tall, lean, and lithe lean man in uniform. Markus recognized him as a Captain in the Spanish Army. A step behind was a short, stocky Teniente, or Lieutenant, followed by a dozen or so other soldiers.

Markus stiffened even more and Aislinn's inquisitive smile faded as the Teniente leered at Aislinn. The Captain, on the other hand, was concentrating on Markus. He strode up to the three, a scowl on his face. "Who are you, and why are you here?"

With the Teniente still leering at Aislinn, she eased slightly behind Markus, and Morgana was moving forward to stand by her side.

Markus made a slight, very slight, bow, more a nod than anything. "I am Markus Lynch, with my sister and her maid. My business is private, with no need for military involvement. And who are you, exactly, Captain?"

"I, Señor Lynch, am Capitán Padilla, Commander of St. Augustine Fort. And it is I that will determine if your business is of interest to the military. And even if you are to stay and conduct any business at all."

Before Markus could respond, a priest hurried over to join them. "Capitán Padilla! Good sir! It is good you and your men have come. It is always good for our community for the military to show that they hold the tenants of the Church in high regard."

Markus noted the Capitán preen a bit at the praise and attention. Markus eased Aislinn and Morgana away, though noted the Teniente's beady pig eyes still on Aislinn. He also noticed that Morgana was very close to attacking the Teniente for his inappropriate and rude appraisal of her charge.

After they seated themselves in the Mission, near the back in an inconspicuous position, Markus watched as the military troop marched inside and took their seats, stacking their weapons in the rack at the door. Except, Markus noted, both the Capitán and the Teniente, along with three Sargentos, kept pistols and swords on their belts.

Morgana shifted slightly to shield Aislinn from the continued perusal the Teniente was again giving the woman. Aislinn was totally ignoring his attention, easily talking to many of the local women after the service was over, with Morgana hovering, never letting Aislinn out of her sight or away from her protection.

Even Markus was more relaxed, talking to several of the men of St. Augustine, including several businessmen that dealt in maritime products. Of course, they could not actually discuss business on Sunday, but Markus was able to find out what he needed to know, as to who he would be calling on the following day.

When Markus caught sight of Capitán Padilla out of the corner of his eyes, Markus signaled the youth holding their horses to bring them forward. Morgana, just as aware of the two men as Markus, kept watch as Markus lifted Aislinn onto Spirit, then mounted her gelding, ready when Markus was to leave the Mission.

Markus could tell that Capitán Padilla and Teniente Chavez were both very unhappy that the three were slipping away from them. Markus vowed then to have as little to do with the Spanish military as possible while the travelers were in Florida.

Markus was correct about the Capitán and the Teniente. Both were more than a little unhappy with the group. Capitán Padilla lost no time in sending some of his spies to find where the group was staying and everything they could about them.

Capitán Padilla already had formed the basics of a plan by the time Markus was leading his people back to Georgia, minus everything they had brought to sell to test the commercial waters in Florida.

Just as Markus was implementing plans to begin shipping maritime chandlery to St. Augustine by sea, down the Big Satilla River into St. Andrew Sound on the Georgia Atlantic coast, Capitán Padilla was implementing his plan to avoid being sent back to Spain to face charges.

Ricardo, having talked to a few of his relatives that still lived in the St. Augustine area, had done much the same as the Capitán. He had arranged for spies to keep an eye on the Capitán and the Teniente specifically, and the military in general, along with the civilian portions of the government of Florida. It was fortunate that he did so, for, less than two weeks after their return to Georgia, one of Ricardo's cousins showed up at the Lynch estate with a warning for the family.

"Markus," Ricardo said after Markus had admitted him and Hernando and a third man that Markus did not know, into the large office in the library of the estate house. "This is my cousin, Manuel. I believe you need to hear what he has to say."

Markus had learned to trust Ricardo and Hernando, and come to depend on them for not only their work, but for their council as well.

"Yes, of course," Markus replied, gesturing to the leather chairs in front of his massive desk of native Cyprus. "A drink, gentlemen?"

Manuel looked at his cousins, who nodded, so he nodded as well. Markus poured them each a small glass of the port he knew Ricardo and Hernando favored.

When he handed the three men their drinks, he sat down behind the desk with his own, and looked at Ricardo expectantly.

"Markus, Manuel and his family have been keeping an eye on things in St. Augustine on your behalf. What they have learned is not good."

All eyes turned to Manuel. Manuel twisted his hat round and round in his hands as he sat on the edge of the chair. "Sir, you are in great danger. You and your sister."

The other three saw Markus stiffen when Manuel mentioned Aislinn.

"My sister works for one of the Hidalgos… She overheard him telling some of his friends that Capitán Padilla has been recalled to Spain. It seems he had to leave Spain in disgrace. His father, a great Hidalgo in Madrid, bought him a Captaincy for the New World detachment. But now the King wants him back to stand charges for his crime.

"No one seems to know what that is, but the Capitán does not want to go back. He, along with Teniente Chavez, who is also facing charges, these stemming from his treatment of some of the women in St. Augustine on church grounds, is deserting. With over one hundred fifty of the soldiers they control, they are coming here, to take over your grounds and make you work them, for them. And…"

Manuel paused, looking at Markus intensely.

"Yes, Manuel? What is the rest?" Markus asked.

"Chavez… He is a brute. He claims your sister as his own. That he will tame her…"

The other three men heard the slight growl from Markus at that, but gave no notice of it. Manuel continued, "They were within a week of leaving when I left St. Augustine. That was six weeks ago. So, they are probably on their way."

Markus nodded. "I see." He cut his eyes over to Ricardo. "See to your cousin's needs. I will consider this, and what should be done." He looked back at Manuel. "Thank you and your family very much. I know this has been a danger to them, and to you. I will not forget it."

Manuel nodded and stood, as did his cousins. Markus was lost in thought as the three men left.

Markus knew he had to let Aislinn know what was happening. Rather reluctantly he went looking for his sister. As he expected, he found her and Morgana in one of the gardens, practicing their swordsmanship. Markus had long ago given up trying to get his sister to be more of a traditional woman and less the pioneer.

He did have to admit that she could ride as well as most men, was as good of a marksman if not better than he, and though she could not best him when they crossed swords, she was very good. She had surpassed Morgana's skill long ago, though Morgana could still give her a very good sparring session.

Markus stopped and watched the two women. Though his thoughts had been on her accomplishments of the more manly pursuits, they turned to her equally excellent womanly skills now. She was an excellent cook, and insisted on doing some of the cooking despite their excellent live in cook and housekeeper.

Modesta had a large family and was often needed at home to help with one of her daughters or grandchildren. When she could not be at the estate, Aislinn would do the cooking for herself, him and Morgana. The workers had their own cook and cleaning woman that shared a cottage on the property with Modesta and three other female servants that lived on-site.

Morgana spotted Markus first and signaled Aislinn. Morgana bowed slightly to Markus, then moved away as Aislinn joined her brother at the edge of the gardens.

"You look troubled, my brother," Aislinn said, flexing the rapier in her hands as her eyes searched Markus' face.

"Trouble, Aislinn."

"How serious, and what shall we do to deflect it?" Aislinn asked, with the innocent and absolute belief in a brother that she considered as near perfect as a sibling could be.

Markus noticed Aislinn's petite nose wrinkle in disgust when Markus relayed Manuel's information about Chavez' interest in her. It never occurred to him not to tell her everything, unlike the way women were often treated and kept in the dark about serious matters, since he not only knew she was capable of dealing with the information, would not swoon in alarm and would quite likely have some good advice to give him on how to handle things.

Morgana trailed along silently, several steps behind the two as Markus and Aislinn discussed the matter as they reentered the house and went to the library to continue talk about options.

"Will not the Spanish authorities stop Capitán Padilla from doing this? They have no authority here any longer," Aislinn said.

Markus sighed and shook his head. "It would be months before Spain could send anyone that would have both the authority and ability to stop Padilla. If what Manuel Estrada said is true, and I have no reason to doubt it, Padilla has at least seventy-five and as many as one hundred fifty men at arms following him. Many of them the dregs of the soldiers' ranks."

"And the English authorities here in Georgia? Would they not take offense to a Spanish Army Officer coming into their lands without permission?"

"They will take great offense," Markus replied. He chuckled without humor. "But what are they to do about it? There are no troops close, and by the time we could get word to anyone that could send word to those that have the power to intervene, it will be too late. We will have to decide how to deal with this on our own, and quickly."

"Our people will fight," Aislinn said proudly. "They are loyal to us. And most hate the Spaniards, even if many are of Spanish heritage."

Markus sighed. "I know. And that worries me."

Both Aislinn and Morgana gave Markus sharp looks.

"How so, brother? Is that not a very good thing?"

Shaking his head, Markus sighed again and dropped into the chair behind his desk. "No. They are loyal and they would fight as best they could. But though we have good weapons for ourselves, and some for them, most would not have anything effective against a trained army detachment's weapons and tactics.

"We… They… would lose, and then the Spaniards would retaliate severely against not only anyone that fought against them, but their families as well. You know how they are. The horror stories from the time they were here before and how they treated the Indians and those Spanish that married with the locals."

It was Aislinn's turn to sigh. Indeed, she had heard from many of the workers' families that Aislinn often helped with medical and children's issues of the atrocities they had suffered under the iron fisted Spaniards.

"So, what do we do, Markus?"

"I am getting a glimmering of an idea… that might just work, depending on just how much pride Padilla might have."

Despite Aislinn's attempts to get Markus to explain further, he refused and sent her and Morgana off for the evening. Markus did not stay up very long himself. He went to bed, letting his mind work on the problem as he slept.

Though Markus had informed Aislinn of the situation and solicited her thoughts, he was still the elder brother, and the decisions to be made were his to make. The next morning Markus was up even earlier than usual, consulting with Ricardo.

It was the first time Ricardo had ever raised his voice, much less contradicted Markus on anything, other than presenting alternatives to Markus' suggestions. This time Ricardo was adamant that he, his brother, and almost all of the other hands would stand with Markus and fight the Spaniards. That they could and would defeat them.

It took all of Markus' patience to talk Ricardo out of the idea when he threatened to gather the men and do it despite Markus' instructions not to do so.

"Ricardo, if my plan works, that will be the end of it. If it does not work, I will not have all of you, and your families put into the position of being direct enemies of Padilla, where he considers you a threat to him and his goals. He would seek you all out, and your families, and destroy all of you. I will not have that on my conscious."

Ricardo finally agreed. He willingly accepted the assignment to keep Aislinn safe at all costs, no matter what might happen to Markus in the ensuing days.

Later that day, one of the locals was sent on a mission to intercept Capitán Padilla and his men to give Padilla a written message. Three days later the man returned and gave Markus the paper on which Padilla had penned his response.

Markus told Ricardo what he needed him to do then reluctantly went to tell Aislinn what he was about to do. She would not be happy. He was sure of it.

He was correct in his assumption. Aislinn was fit to be tied. "I will not allow it! Markus, you will not fight a duel with Padilla! I forbid it! We will fight! All of us!"

"You would have Modesta and her family killed for a few horses and a house, Aislinn?" Markus asked quietly when Aislinn finally quit ranting at him.

He winced when Aislinn went deathly pale and stared at him with huge eyes, tears gathering in the corners. "No! I would never..." she whispered; her voice barely perceptible.

"I know, Aislinn. I know. I am sorry. I should not have said that. But it is what would happen. I am sure of it. The more I learn of Padilla and Chavez, if I do not win that duel, it is a lost cause here. So, make ready to leave, and ready the staff that chooses not to stay to leave with you if the Spaniards take over.

"Ricardo and Hernando are doing the same with the field and stable workers. Be ready the day after tomorrow to go into hiding until the outcome is decided, and if I do not return by the day after that, you are to go to the coast, take passage on a ship to Boston, and contact our solicitor there."

Aislinn opened her mouth to protest, but closed it quickly and said nothing. She nodded, but her mind was already at work on a plan of her own.

Satisfied, at least nominally, that his plan was being followed, Markus took the rest of the day to go out into the wilderness to calm himself, contemplate the future and try to come up with any type of an alternate plan.

Nothing had come to him by the time he rode out to meet with Padilla and Chavez. Nor was he all that surprised to see Ricardo, Hernando, Morgana and, of course, Aislinn sitting astride horses at the edge of the clearing where Markus was to duel with Padilla.

It was obvious Aislinn was going to ride forward to meet him, but Markus held up a hand, and Ricardo and Morgana both moved to block Aislinn's horse. Hernando did ride forward to take the reins of Markus' stallion after he dismounted in the center of the grassy clearing.

Chavez had done the same for Padilla, taking the reins of his horse and leading him back to the other side of the clearing. Markus' Spanish was fluent, and he asked Padilla, "You are clear on this, Sir? If I defeat you in a fair sword fight, you will turn around and leave Georgia with your men and take no further action against me, my family, or my estates."

"That is the agreement," Padilla said. "I am an Officer. I shall do what is right."

Markus did not like Padilla's words, but there was little choice but to continue with the duel. Both men threw off their tunics and drew their swords. A salute with sword raised to their face, and then both went into a ready stance.

It was very obvious from Padilla's initial moves that he expected Markus to be a mediocre swordsman. But Markus surprised Padilla. Long before he had left Ireland, Markus had been a well-trained swordsman. And he had continued his practice after arriving in the New World.

They fought for over ten minutes, with point and counterpoint, thrust and parry, until Padilla made a small mistake and Markus was able to cut Padilla's sword arm slightly. It seemed to infuriate Padilla, and he went into a flurry of attacks, slashing and thrusting wildly.

All it did was allow Markus to slip past several times and prick Padilla time after time. Markus was still untouched when Padilla made another wild lunge, and Markus was able to run his sword deep into Padilla's upper right thigh.

Markus withdrew the sword and stepped back. Padilla went down, dropping his sword. Chavez ran forward and dropped to one knee beside his commanding officer.

"It is over, Padilla," Markus said. "Leave this area and do not come back." Markus cut his eyes to Chavez. "And you will remove all thoughts of my sister from your head."

Markus sheathed his sword, picked up his tunic and walked over to join Aislinn and the others. His shoulders slumped and Ricardo helped him to mount Leprechaun. The five rode off without exchanging a word.

Padilla and Chavez, however, were far from silent. Padilla cursed for a long time as Chavez tended the wound in the Capitán's leg. Chavez talked less but was just as adamant about his plans for Aislinn. There was no mention at all of Padilla honoring the terms of the duel. It never even occurred to Chavez that Padilla would not pursue his goal of taking over the Lynch operation.

It crossed Padilla's mind, for a tiny fraction of a second, that his father would be even more disappointed in him than he already was for his lack of honor in this. But it was a fleeting thought. He had no honor and he knew it. He knew what he wanted, and the only way he was going to get it was by taking it from those who had it.

Finally, Chavez got Padilla back on his horse and the two headed for their encampment, already modifying their plans on how to take over the Lynch estate and what they would do with it once it was under their control.

While Markus was in the process of getting back to business as usual, Padilla rested and recovered as Chavez got their men ready to move again and get ready for the attack as planned.

Again, Ricardo's foresight and distrust of the Spaniards paid off. As soon as the man he had assigned to keep an eye on the rogue Spanish military unit reported that they had begun to move once more, still on track to arrive at the Lynch property within the week, Ricardo took him to talk to Markus.

"We have at most three days to be ready to fight, Señor Lynch. I believe…"

Markus interrupted his foreman. "No, Ricardo. We will not fight."

Ricardo could see the strain that Markus was under. Obviously, the decision did not come easily to the man.

"We could not win. And would only get good people killed for no gain. You must convince our people to cooperate with Padilla, else they risk far too much. You know how the Spaniards treat people that oppose them. Especially natives. Aislinn and I will simply leave. Start over somewhere else.

"I will give everyone enough to be able to leave if they choose or have in reserve if they choose to stay. I do not want anyone put at risk or suffer due to my actions."

Ricardo protested, but he soon gave up, another plan coming to his mind. "Yes Sir. You are probably correct, Señor. I shall take care of everything. You just take care of yourself and your sister. Do not worry about the rest of us. You have provided well."

Markus wondered for a moment at Ricardo's sudden acquiescence, but Ricardo did tend to make snap decisions, after due deliberation. Markus thought no more of it and when Ricardo left, he went about convincing Aislinn to go along with the plan.

He had as much trouble convincing her as he had convincing Ricardo. But finally, after Morgana did essentially the same thing as Ricardo, switching from wanting to fight to going along with Markus' plan, Aislinn agreed to do so as well. But she made it clear she was not happy with the decision.

Once the decisions had been made, they were carried out quickly. Ricardo made sure that Morgana, Aislinn, and especially Markus, had no clue to what his own plan actually was. When Markus astride Leprechaun, and Aislinn on Spirit, rode through the gates of the estate with Morgana driving one of the heavy transport wagons, with another half a dozen horses strung out behind on long lead ropes, Ricardo turned back to the staff gathered to say good-bye to the Lynches.

The staff looked at Ricardo silently for a few moments, and then he began to issue orders. All hurried to obey, for they knew the consequences if they did not follow through with Ricardo's plan. When the Spaniards arrived and found what they would find, anyone left in the area would suffer greatly.

Even though he had not mentioned it, Markus did not fully trust Padilla so he was very careful as they headed east, toward the Atlantic Ocean. Markus' plan was to head for Boston and restructure their finances. Then they would start over somewhere else.

Despite the losses leaving the estate would create, Markus and Aislinn were even better off financially than they were when they first came to the New World, so he was not worried. It rankled nonetheless, leaving the way he was. He was one to stand up for himself and what was right. Even stronger was his belief in preserving the life and well-being of people. He simply was not willing to risk the people that he had come to consider more than just employees. They were like family to him, now.

It was well that Markus was scouting ahead every so often. For he was right not to trust Padilla. Markus saw at least twenty men waiting just off the road to the coast not more than forty miles from the Lynch estate.

He considered the options open to them as he quickly rode back to join Aislinn and Morgana where they had stopped to prepare a noon meal.

When he explained what he had seen there was very little argument when he said they would turn south. Going north at the moment was out the question due to the swampy terrain. Hopefully they could swing south for a few miles and then cut back toward the Atlantic.

Whoever was in charge of the blocking detachment was smarter than many of the other officers and non-commissioned officers with Padilla and Chavez. Markus, Aislinn, and Morgana were able to continue to evade capture, but the Spaniards were able to continue to force them south, with no chance to turn back to the east.

After a week of constant movement Markus discussed it with Aislinn and they decided to just head the rest of the way into Florida and get a ship there to take them north.

With the decision made, Markus set a fast pace and after three more days the Spaniards were no longer tracking them. Apparently, they went to join with Padilla and Chavez, leaving the Lynches and Morgana to their fate.

Though he was worried about those he had left behind, he tried to not dwell on it. And he hated the fact that he had made the choice to leave and refuse to fight. He was relieved that not one of his people had been hurt due to his actions.

Upon their arrival in St. Augustine, the first thing Markus did after getting Aislinn and Morgana settled in suitable accommodations, was to visit the Spanish military headquarters.

First, he got the runaround when he attempted to lodge an official complaint. Finally, he did get an audience with the Governor General which did very little to satisfy him. The Governor General was not even very apologetic about what Padilla and Chavez were doing.

"It is outside my jurisdiction," Markus was told. "It is a matter for the Crown to resolve."

Markus did get assurance that his complaint would be sent through channels to Spain. He had his doubts, but left it at that. Everyone was all right, and that was his main concern. He went back to join Aislinn and settle in for a few days while they made arrangements to get a ship to Boston.

Of course, Aislinn insisted on going with him everywhere, and where Aislinn went, Morgana went. Which meant that the three were on their way back from the port, where they had been making inquiries about outbound ships, when Aislinn sudden stopped walking and went very still.

Morgana and Markus noticed at the same instant and while Morgana checked her charge for injuries, Markus, his hand on one of pistols, looked around for whatever might have caught her attention.

There was no one anywhere close and Markus leaned down slightly and looked into Aislinn's green eyes. They seemed glazed, and Aislinn totally lost in thought.

Markus touched Aislinn's arm and she started. "Markus!" she gasped.

"Aislinn, are you alright? You went… silent… or something."

"I… something…" Aislinn said, slowly coming back into full awareness. She looked around for a moment and then focused on a track that led from the road toward the ocean.

"There…" she said, pointing in that direction.

"What?" Markus asked, still concerned.

"There," she said again, still pointing. "Something… There is something we should see…" She started walking in that direction, seeming to lose touch with her surroundings again.

Morgana looked at Markus with concern. "Sir?" Suddenly she added, "There is… something…" Her eyes, as had Aislinn's, lost focus, but only for a moment. "We must go."

"We shall see what is drawing her. Be ready for… Well… Anything."

Both hurried after Aislinn, one taking up a position on each side of her. Both knew that Aislinn was fae, but it had never been very active in her. Both had a feeling that it was her abilities that were controlling her now. And Morgana was feeling it, too, though it was somewhat weaker in her.

After a fair walk down the track, they broke through the forest they were going through and came upon a shipbuilding operation. There was no one around as Aislinn continued to walk, now focused on a storage area that contained large stacks of timbers.

Markus was beginning to look closely at the timbers when Aislinn stopped and looked at Markus. "Ours…" she said, pointing at the stacks.

Moving closer, Markus checked several the largest timbers. Indeed, they did carry the Lynch product identification marks. He turned to look at Aislinn. She seemed still under the influence of whatever it was that was connected with her being fae.

"They are upset… They do not want to be here… They were… taken."

Markus looked confused. "Taken? They were taken?"

Aislinn did not say anything for a moment, but then her eyes refocused and she was looking at Markus, back to her normal self. "Markus? Um… I'm not sure… What was it I said?"

Morgana relaxed slightly, but kept a wary eye on Aislinn.

"You said something about the timbers being taken. That they do not want to be here?"

Aislinn thought for a moment and then nodded. "Yes. I feel it now. Not like… before. But this," she said, her hand sweep encompassing everything there in the clearing, "isn't right somehow."

"This is the shipment for Escobar. But why would it be here?" Markus looked confused.

At the sound of a shout, all three spun around and looked toward the path. Four men were running toward them, one still shouting. Markus had a difficult time understanding the rapid-fire Spanish.

When the four men came up, Morgana had moved beside Markus, trying to keep Aislinn behind her. Aislinn was having none of it. She wanted to know just what was going on as much as Markus did.

Finally, Markus got the apparent leader of the four men calmed down enough so he could understand him. Markus stiffened almost immediately when the man ordered them to leave the area. It was a Spanish Navy site storing the materials to build a new brigantine to combat piracy.

Markus had sold the timbers to Escobar specifically for civilian ships, having made the decision not to sell to the Spaniards for warships. He cut the man off abruptly, and motioned to Aislinn and Morgana to head for the path.

He followed them silently, fuming at what he had learned. Even Morgana had a difficult time keeping up with Markus as he headed back to the main part of the port.

When they reached the Escobar offices, Markus was quickly informed that the Spanish Governor General had confiscated the timbers Markus had shipped, along with the rest of the primary materials for a brigantine and other ships from several other of the shipbuilders and chandlers in St. Augustine.

Escobar was obviously angry, but he was also obviously not going to challenge the Spanish authorities. A sudden idea came to Markus and he fell silent, looking thoughtful for a moment before he turned and left the building, Aislinn and Morgana right on his heels.

Aislinn knew Markus very well. "What is it, Markus? You have something in mind."

Morgana kept quiet, but she too could tell Markus' mind was working.

"Let me think," he said quietly, as they headed back to their accommodations.

Aislinn nodded. Markus would confide in her when he had thought through whatever it was he was thinking about. It was not until late that evening that Markus asked to talk to Aislinn.

"I have come to a decision, Aislinn. One you will question, but I ask that you accept what I am going to do without argument. I want you to go to Boston, just as we planned. I trust Morgana to get you there safely, where you can establish a home for yourself. I am going to stay here for a while and have a ship built. And then I am going to make the Spanish regret they ever had Capitán Padilla and Teniente Chavez in their service, or the Governor General."

Aislinn's temper flared, but, much to Markus' surprise, she did not explode. Instead, she asked, "How are you going to, as you put it, make the Spanish regret what they have done? And what does building a ship have to do with it?"

Markus looked away for a moment. He It did not take him long to figure out it was better to get it out now. Aislinn would figure it out eventually. And knowing might just help convince her that going to Boston would be her best, and safest, option.

"I am going to become a pirate, Aislinn. Take the Escobar timbers back, and take all the rest from where it is stored, and take it somewhere and built a pirate ship. I will find a crew and prey on the Spanish Treasure Galleons, until they do something about Padilla and the Governor General. Stop their terrible treatment of the people here."

"I see," Aislinn said softly, studying the hard lines of Markus' face. She had seen him upset several times, occasionally at her, but never anything like this since they had left Ireland when he was so upset with their father. Making a quick decision herself, Aislinn put a soft hand on Markus' arm.

"I understand, Markus. This is something you obviously believe you must do. I will not protest your plans. I will do whatever you need me to do in order to further the completion of the ship and get it, with you at the helm, onto the seas to exact our revenge and punish the Spaniards."

More than a little surprised, Markus took Aislinn's hand into his. "Thank you, Sister. This means much to me. I just cannot let these injustices go without doing something about them. It is probably not my wisest choice of action, but I feel that the risks are worth what I may accomplish. And I assure you that I will not harm anyone unnecessarily. But I will take those Galleons and what they carry. And make sure the Spanish Crown knows who is taking what they consider theirs, and why."

Aislinn nodded, and slid her hand from his. "That is good, Markus. Justice must be obtained, and people will die, but I trust you that you will not abuse your power, once you have it."

"Thank you, Aislinn. I am glad you understand. Now, go to your bed. I still have to plan the taking of the timbers and other things. I will be out for some time. Do not worry about me. I will be back some time tomorrow."

Again, Aislinn held her tongue. She smiled very slightly. Markus really did not understand just what she had agreed to do. She would let him continue to think she was going to do what he thought she was, while forming her own plans.

She stood and left to go to her room, with Markus leaving the house sometime later.

For three days Aislinn kept quiet and let Markus go off and do whatever it was he was doing. However, when they were ready to start the day on the fourth day, Aislinn stopped him. "What is going on, Markus? It is time you told me what you are doing."

Reluctantly, Markus decided that he was not going to be able to keep Aislinn in the dark any longer. Perhaps, once she knew that he was actually following through on the basic plan he had told her about, she would agree to go to Boston. Every time he had brought it up the last three days, she had simply ignored him.

So, Markus nodded. "Get ready for a day in the field. I will show you what is going on."

With an impish grin, Aislinn nodded and then hurried off, Morgana right on her heels. Markus sighed and did a little planning in his head, taking a few notes as he did. As always, Aislinn was ready very quickly, as she usually was. It was one of the things he really appreciated about his sister.

When Aislinn and Morgana were ready, and the horses were saddled, Markus led them out of St. Augustine, going south on the main road. Aislinn was rather surprised they traveled so far before Markus turned off the road and headed for the Atlantic Ocean shore.

She heard the activity long before they reached the small bay, nearly surrounded with trees. There was a dock running out into the bay for a short distance. There was a beehive of activity going on as the ship tied up to the dock was being loaded.

Immediately Aislinn rode up beside Markus. "Those are our timbers! The ones the Spaniards had! How… What… What is going on, Markus?"

Markus sighed. "I really did not want you to be involved in any of this, Aislinn. But it is just as I said. I made a few inquiries and found a ship and captain that would smuggle us and the ship materials the Spaniards confiscated to Savanah."

Hastily he added, "I gave Escobar his money back, as well as paid the others from whom the Spaniards had confiscated items. The items the Spaniards furnished themselves… well, they are just the first installment of what I plan to do to them."

"I never really doubted you doing what you said, Markus. But I wasn't completely sure. Now I am. When do we leave for Savanah?"

Again Markus sighed. He knew this fight was coming, and he dreaded it. "You, sister dear, are going to Boston, just as we discussed."

"We did not discuss it, Markus! You simply said it. I never agreed to it and I never will. I am just as affected by all of this as you are. Perhaps more so. Teniente Chavez…" Aislinn shivered slightly.

"Do not even try to dissuade me, Markus. I am going, and that is that!" She stood there, the breeze from the ocean stirring her fiery red hair, her hands fisted on her hips, glaring at him.

Markus stared at his sister for a long time, trying to think of a way to make her change her mind. Or come up with a plan to slip away without her knowing. After a bit he realized that even if he did get away from her, she would either follow, and risk more danger than going with him, or would wind up in some kind of trouble here, if Padilla sent someone back to Florida looking for them.

Very, very reluctantly Markus nodded. "Very well, sister. You may go with me to Savanah. But then you will be going to Boston. There is no way you will be going on the ship with me once it is completed."

Aislinn simply nodded in acceptance. She would deal with whether or not she went on the ship once built later. No need to give Markus any time to come up with a plan to prevent it. "Thank you, Brother," she said, rather sweetly. "You have made a wise and considerate decision. Now tell me what I will need to pack to take with us, and how much time I have to get ready."

"I will check with the Captain and see how much longer it will take for them to be ready. We took everything from the Spaniard storage spot at once, but it is hidden about in many places. They are moving it only as much as they can load in a day, and then sail out to stand off the coast so the Spanish patrols will not find them.

"This bay is a favorite smuggler and pirate landing, and so far the Spaniards have not discovered it, but the Captain is a cautious man. And I agree with his caution."

As soon as Markus rode the rest of the way over to the dock, Aislinn and Morgana dismounted. They began to discuss what they would need for the trip. Aislinn never doubted that Morgana would go with them. And the thought never entered Morgana's head that she would not go.

It turned out that they only had two days to get ready. They were to sail on the third day, but there were several things that happened in those two days that both surprised Markus, worried him, and made him feel rather blessed.

Ricardo and Hernando Estrada both showed up and contacted Markus when he was making arrangements to sell, reluctantly, most of the horses they had brought with them. They would only be able to take their three primary mounts. And the ship's captain was not happy about that. Though, less reluctant about the horses than about the fact that there would be two women on his ship.

"Ricardo!" Markus exclaimed when Ricardo softly called Markus' name from where he stood at the corner of the stable building.

"Sir, if you will?" Ricardo said, motioning him to follow. Since Markus still had not been able to make any legitimate deal for the sale of the horses, he followed Ricardo.

When Markus tried to ask Ricardo what was going on, Ricardo put a finger to his lips for silence. Markus simply followed as Ricardo moved quickly thorough the forest. It was with more than a bit of surprise when they came to the road and Markus found not only Leprechaun, but Ricardo's brother Hernando, and an even dozen of the former Lynch employees.

"What is going on, Ricardo? Why are you and these men here?" Markus asked.

"We are here to work, Señor. For you. After we made sure the families were set up safely, we followed you and the Lady. We will not work for the Spanish bastards, and we, Hernando and I, believe that you have a plan to get back at them in some way."

Markus was shaking his head. "You cannot, Ricardo. It is too dangerous, what I plan to do. And... I do not want to hurt your feelings, but I do not think you would be much help, anyway."

Hernando grinned as Ricardo smiled and said, "You might be surprised, Markus. We are not all simple farmers and cattlemen and wood cutters. I take it this involves a ship in some way."

Markus nodded.

Hernando motioned for five of the men to step forward from the group. Ricardo grinned and told Markus, "These five are expert sailors, thanks to the Spanish Navy. No less than three years, and as much as ten in service before leaving the Navy, for one reason or another."

"And you know how well we adapt and learn quickly new tasks," Hernando added proudly. Markus had often said that very thing to them over the years.

"Yes. Yes, I know," Markus said. "But… What I am doing could very well get you hanged. That will most likely be my fate. But I do intend to make trouble for the Spaniards, every chance I get. And that includes pirating their treasure galleons, and smuggling goods in and out of their territories. We will undoubtedly be in, hopefully not too frequently, ship to ship battles, as well as fighting on land."

Ricardo turned and made sure all the men understood what Markus had said. Most had learned quite a bit of English, even a bit of Gaelic, just as Aislinn and Markus had learned Spanish, but there were nuances that Ricardo wanted to make sure the men understood.

Markus noted two men having a quick, quiet discussion. Both suddenly nodded to each other, caught Ricardo's eye and nodded at him. Ricardo turned back to Markus. "All understand and wish to accompany you, wherever you may go."

"Your families? I know some of you have families. You can't just up and leave them unprotected," Markus insisted.

All the men were shaking their heads. Ricardo smiled and explained. "We are not the only ones that followed, Markus. Our families, and even some of the extended family members came as well. We have set up a large farm well outside of St. Augustine where the families will stay.

"There are more than enough men and older boys to keep everyone safe. And to run the farm to support them while we are away. We do expect to come back. But will risk what we must to see this endeavor through."

Markus was again shaking his head. "It is too much responsibility…"

Ricardo interrupted Markus, something he almost never did. "Sir, you and your sister have brought great things to our families and our community in Georgia. It made no difference to either of you any of our heritage, be it local, Spanish, English, French, or any of the others that are in the mix. You are a good man, treat people fairly, and are caring, and generous to a fault. We feel honored to be able to assist you."

Markus stared at the men. All looked at him with pride and eagerness in their eyes. He gave one slight nod and the men gave a rousing cheer. As they headed toward the families' farm, Markus explained to Ricardo and Hernando his plan, in detail.

Every once in a while, Ricardo and Hernando would exchange a glance, but neither seemed too surprised, nor at all reluctant to follow the plan.

Aislinn got tears in her eyes when Markus showed up with Ricardo and greeted him, after Markus explained the situation. "You are loyal, and our friends. We do not want any harm to come to any of you," Aislinn said earnestly. "Are you sure you want to do this?"

Markus watched, a bit amused, as Ricardo explained again that they wanted to do it. Aislinn was getting a bit of a taste of what she put Markus through from time to time.

"Very well," Aislinn finally said. "So shall it be. I would like to visit the families before we leave, if that would be allowed."

"Of course, Señorita. We would all welcome your visit." Ricardo looked over at Markus. "And we would welcome managing your herds, if you wish, for you. That way you will not have to sell them, nor lose them."

"You would do that?" Markus asked, very pleased with the idea. He really did have hopes of returning, still a free man, and take up where he had left off with his champion horses and cattle.

"Of course, Señor," Ricardo said. "Happily. Especially if we might do some breeding of our own."

Markus laughed and slapped Ricardo on the back. "Absolutely, Ricardo. Absolutely."

Ricardo grinned and that was that.

And with that, the course was set. Markus was soon to become Irish Red, Gentleman Pirate of the Caribbean. And the rumors of a beautiful, tiny, redheaded wraith that always seemed to be near him, as well as the rumor of a giantess that was even more fierce and skilled in battle than any other pirate sailing the seas.

CHAPTER THREE

They had no trouble on the trip, despite the fears and superstitions of the sailors on Captain Mellows' ship about having women aboard. By the end of the trip, some of them were rather in awe of Morgana, including Captain Mellow. Not just for her size and obvious fierceness about protecting Aislinn, but her very unexpected talent of laying the guns the Gwendolyn carried.

Despite vehement protests from several of the men, Morgana joined them on the gun deck of the Gwendolyn both times they did short gunnery drills. Since Markus wanted to learn, as did several of his men, and Aislinn was just curious, and Morgana was not going to allow her to go anywhere she did not, Morgana was watching with the others as the Gwendolyn gun crews trained a couple of sailors new to their crew.

Morgana's fascination with weapons of war was even more acute than Markus' practical one. As soon as the first cannon went off, Morgana was right there as the next one was prepared to fire. Fortunately, for everyone's sake, one of the gunners did not share the superstitions of his shipmates and was agreeable to allowing Morgana to become a temporary member of his crew.

It was not unexpected to see her prowess of handling the various aspects of maneuvering, loading, and running the cannon out to fire. She was, after all, a very large and strong woman. That was obvious, and the men had seen her helping hoist the passengers' belongings aboard.

When the gunner let Morgana lay the cannon for its third turn to fire, after he had explained and showed Morgana the techniques the first two rounds, and her shot obliterated the damaged barrel that was the floating target, no one was more surprised than Morgana.

The crew was stunned, and laid it off to absolute, sheer luck. The second time they began to have doubts about her luck. And the third accurate shot had them believing she was actually good at it.

Though, of course, some believed she was a witch and was either making the cannon balls hit the target with a spell on them, or she had everyone bewitched so they saw what she wanted them to see and the cannonballs were flying far off target.

Only Markus and Aislinn wondered if Morgana's fae abilities had anything to do with her ability.

It was a highly embarrassed Morgana that rejoined Aislinn and the others after the gunnery practice was finished. As Markus and the others praised her, she could only reply in Gaelic, unable to remember her English.

Aislinn went back to the tiny cabin she and Morgana shared, a small smile on her face. Morgana's skill with ship's guns was a piece of information that Aislinn might just make use of in the future.

Captain Mellows went well out to sea to reduce the chance of running into Spanish ships that might be looking for the timbers that Markus had taken from them. It was still a fairly quick trip to Savannah, to the same shipbuilding yard that had been his customer since the very beginning. It was not his largest customer, a shipyard in Boston was, but the owner was a good friend.

A nervous Captain Mellows quickly got the Gwendolyn unloaded at the shipyard and set sail once again, happy to get away from the official activity happening in the harbor at Savannah.

Markus had no worries on that score. There was no reason for anyone in Savannah to suspect anything out of the ordinary. Markus, Aislinn, and Morgana had been to the shipyard more than once with a load of their timbers. The only real difference was that they had used the Gwendolyn instead of the usual shippers he used.

That and the fact that the additional people were with them. Markus quickly got them away from the shipyard and in local accommodations before he began discussing the building of the ship he wanted.

Markus attempted to get Aislinn to agree to head for Boston with Morgana, but she was determined to stay and watch the brigantine being constructed. Markus decided he would just wait and when it was time to set sail, then he would, somehow, convince her. He shook his head unconsciously at the thought.

Sean O'Malley was a fellow Irishman, already a good friend, and fortunately for Markus, the O'Malley shipyard was not very busy at the moment. It was also fortunate that Sean also hated the Spaniards with a passion.

Sean had immediately recognized the design that Markus had brought him would be no ordinary merchant brigantine. It was well known by those in the maritime industries what pirates did to the ships they captured or bought to turn them into pirate ships. It was unheard of for a pirate to have the time or means to build a ship from the keel up for pirating.

Less than a week after their arrival, Markus and Sean had finalized the design of the brigantine, including a couple of ideas from Sean, and several of Markus' own. Then the work began, despite the use it would be put to.

Part of the reason Sean went along with it was that he now had another reason to hate the Spaniards. Markus would no longer be able to supply him with the premium timbers and lumber, plus the provisions, which Markus had always sold to him at fair prices. He was going to lose business because of it. Definitely another reason to hate the Spaniards.

Not long after their family's arrival in the New World, when Sean was still young, and his cousin even younger, she was killed by sailors from a Spanish warship. He had been very close to his cousin and her death was devastating to him.

Though only ten at the time, Sean was already plotting his revenge, but the Spaniards retreated from Georgia to their strongholds in Florida long before he was of an age to actually do anything.

Though somewhat reluctant at first, it did not take Sean long to decide that having Markus' men work with his on the ship was not going to be the disaster he first assumed.

All of Markus' employees were hard workers, to start with, and intelligent, able to pick up more than enough skills to be of major help. And several of them, Sean and his crews found, were already fairly skilled in several of the techniques of ship building.

More surprisingly, after even stronger objections than Markus' men working on the ship, Sean and his men quit complaining about Aislinn and Morgana being around. At first, just their curious natures and interest in so many different things had them walking around, watching, and asking the occasional question.

Since nothing happened, despite the strong superstitions about women and ships, just as it had been on the Gwendolyn, Sean's men shortly quit complaining and avoiding them. They even started not only answering their questions, but would offer up information on what they were doing, and why, whenever they were around.

Of course, Morgana was always with Aislinn, and it had quickly become clear that Morgana was like a tiger with a cub about Aislinn, and it was just as obvious that Markus' men would give their lives to protect her, and rain havoc on any man that acted inappropriately toward not only Aislinn, but Morgana, who was a bit more at risk as she was in the working class in their eyes.

As the ship was built, everyone in Markus' group learned every detail about it from the keel to the topmast, and everything in between. Plus, those of Markus' employees that had come from the estate that did not have experience in sailing, no matter their skills with timbers, were getting a very good basic education on how a ship was sailed. And the workings of everything on board, including the cannon.

And excellent cannon they were. Markus had no idea how the Spaniards had acquired them, for they were of the latest British Admiralty design manufactured in England. There were far more of them than a brigantine would normally carry, so Markus and Sean thought that they were meant for more than one ship, and simply had been stored together with the stolen timbers and other items for ship building.

Even with the extra armament that the brigantine would carry, there would be many of the cannon left at the ship building yard. The extra cannon and the other gear that Markus would not need that had been liberated from the Spaniards would be part of the payment that Sean would receive,

There were twenty twenty-four-pounders, sixteen eighteen-pounders, sixteen twelve-pounders, eight Long Nine nine-pounders, and a multitude of other, smaller cannon. All of the cannon were well made bronze versions, even the Long Nines, which was unusual now due to the better cast iron available, and much higher expense of bronze.

Apparently, the Admiralty had apparently wanted the best of the best for whatever use they had for them. Most of the smaller cannon were also bronze, but there were a few of cast iron as well.

Even in bronze, the twenty-four-pounder cannon were too heavy to have more than six of them on board. They were on the gun deck amidships, three each port and starboard. Two each of the eighteen-pounders were fore and aft of the twenty-fours, port and starboard. That gave fourteen guns on the gun deck.

The top deck had two Long Nines as bow chase guns, and two as aft chase guns, plus six twelve-pounders, three each port and starboard amidships. With the ten guns on the top deck, the brigantine was very well armed with twenty-four rated guns.

Where railing space allowed, there were one and a half inch bore bronze swivel cannon every few feet, giving the Irish Rose's crew extremely good anti-personnel capability against anyone on the exposed decks of any ship in close range.

Even the five long boats the ship would carry were armed with two swivel guns, one each fore and aft. Just the fact that there would be five long boats was unusual, but having them armed was even more so. As were the way they were equipped, capable of sailing very well, in addition to the oars.

Some of the other pirate specific design features of the brigantine included the flush top deck rather than having raised fore and aft decks, which kept the ship much lighter. Below decks were much more open than normal, in the pirate ship manner, which also lightened the weight of the ship.

However, where often the only cabin below decks was that of the Captain, there were some other cabins besides the Captain's cabin below, including one set up as the ship's surgery.

And while Markus had no intention of Aislinn being aboard, a cabin was incorporated suited for her and Morgana, just to avoid any arguments.

The brigantine was rather longer than usual, with a slightly narrower beam. She was built with over size heavy oak hull timbers, well reinforced with more and thicker than usual oak hull planking.

Her two masts, both taller and heavier than normal for a brigantine, carried appropriately heavier spars and rigging. She would be able to carry a very large sail area, making her a very fast ship.

However, still being lighter than normal for even a brigantine, especially of her size, she would be able to navigate shallow water. The much lighter weight of the bronze cannon over cast iron contributed to that capability.

As there was not all that much need for a great deal of bulky cargo space, the gun deck was lower in the ship than usual, and even with the additional armament on the top deck, the ship was very stable.

It still left the bottom deck with more than enough room for the ballast and any cargo they would have, plus room for additional munitions and stores, giving them the capability of long times at sea without resupply. It also made moving about on the gun deck much easier, with its higher head clearance.

It also facilitated the most unusual for the times addition of rowing ports and oars, with seating that could be easily stowed when not in use, and almost as quickly mounted and the oars rigged.

Oars on brigantines had been common in centuries past. They were not in favor now, at least in the Atlantic Ocean. The oars would not be used as a primary means of propulsion, but would be shipped if caught in a calm, or they had to maneuver in a port when there was little or no wind, or it was counter to what was needed to handle the ship the way that was wanted. Markus got more than a few worrisome looks when he ordered the modification and it was being implemented.

Had a third mast been added, which was discussed, the brigantine could easily have been considered a barkentine. It was decided to simply use the heavier, larger masts and their associated larger sail area, rather than add the complications of a third mast.

Even being larger than the brigantines of the time, along with the other changes, being much lighter than she looked, she was still a brigantine.

While the ship was being built, Ricardo was tasked with the gathering of provisions and everything else they would need for a successful endeavor, except for small arms for the ship's armory. That Markus would take care of right at the end of the construction process, before the sea trials.

Markus was rather proud of his plan to get the arms himself. Massachusetts had many excellent weapons manufacturers and importers. He had early on sent enquiries to several of them, and after receiving replies, had sent off orders with payment.

Markus had always believed that quality was worth the extra amount that it cost. The weapons they had at the Lynch estate were all quality firearms and edged weapons.

Those he ordered to equip the men that would be aboard his pirate ship would be the same. The best that could be had at the time.

There was no problem convincing Aislinn to go along with him. The problem came after they had picked up all the arms and had them shipped to Savanah. That was when Markus turned Leprechaun toward Boston the morning they left. He suddenly noticed that Aislinn and Morgana were nowhere to be seen when he turned to check on them.

Usually a well-spoken man, Markus uttered a curse under his breath, and turned his horse around. Bringing Leprechaun up to a gallop he soon caught up with Aislinn and Morgana, heading south on the road. Morgana, knowing what was coming, rode a discreet distance away with the pack horses when both Markus and Aislinn drew up, side by side.

"Do you really think I am going to stay in Boston while you are out at sea, making the Spaniards pay for what they have done? Did to both you and me, plus all the others? It is my fight, too, Markus. I will be on that ship when it sails for the Caribbean."

Markus continued to talk firmly. It was not an argument, since Aislinn said not a word. She simply sat her horse, listening, her green eyes never leaving Markus' face. He finally fell silent. Giving Aislinn a long look, he shook his head, and flicked Leprechaun's reins, heading him south. Aislinn and Morgana fell in behind him, a gentle smile on Aislinn's face and a slightly worried one on Morgana's.

With only a few exceptions, everything was ready with the brigantine for her sea trials when the three arrived back in Savannah. After a short christening ceremony, where Aislinn named the brigantine Irish Rose, enough provisions were loaded for the time it would take to do the sea trials.

Sean and a couple of his employees joined Markus and his crew for the sea trials, in case something came up that they might need to address that Markus' crew would not be experienced enough to handle.

Though Markus was the Irish Rose's Captain without doubt, he willingly drew upon the knowledge of everyone aboard that had the experience to give him good advice and recommendations.

At the end of the sea trials, Sean told Markus, "You are a natural, Markus. Not only are you good with handling the ship and making sailing decisions, you handle your crew extremely well. Especially with two women aboard." Sean shook his head. "Never thought I'd see the day where women were welcome on a ship as anything except as passengers."

Markus almost told Sean that he intended to see that Aislinn and Morgana would not be sailing with them when the Irish Rose left Savannah for the Caribbean, but held his tongue, not at all sure that would be the case.

Which turned out to have been a good idea, for Aislinn made it very clear that she was going. Markus gave up rather gracefully, and quit trying to dissuade her. Irish Rose was fully provisioned, armed, and otherwise equipped, ready to sail seventy-seven days from the day the keel was set up. Sean said it was a record he was not sure he would ever be able to beat.

Two nights before they were to set sail, Sean asked Markus to meet him at a tavern near the harbor. He would not tell Markus why, but Markus readily agreed. When Markus arrived, Sean was already at a table well in the back of the large place. He was not alone. Three other men sat with him, all with tankards before them.

Markus nodded warily as he joined the men. A barmaid quickly arrived and Markus ordered an ale. Then he turned his eyes to Sean and lifted an eyebrow.

Sean leaned forward slightly, and keeping his voice low, began to talk. "Well, my friend, I know you are highly capable, and a quick learner, but I think it might be well for you to talk to these three old seafarers."

Sean cut his eyes to the oldest of the three men. He had a thick beard, mostly gray, and what hair Markus could see was all gray. His voice was gravelly when he spoke. "I'll not say of what we speak, but be ye sure that I do know of what I shall impart to you, as I have lived it. Many years ago. Many. But things have not changed all that much. Men are still men.

"Ye must write yourself a Ship's Articles. And be firm about it. No quarter asked nie given in execution. Given many a man that work hard and true, if given a firm hand and treated rightly, sail without being troublesome."

The man leaned back and took a long draught from his tankard. Apparently, that was all he had to say at the moment. Markus nodded.

"Aye," said the second man, sitting beside the first. Markus turned his eyes to the man as he continued. "He speaks the truth. But let me warn ye. There are those that will sign, and then incite mutiny at the first chance. Have mates you trust that men will trust, so crewmen will let it be known of trouble quickly, without danger to themselves, for their benefit of more and better prizes with thee, than another. Let not these men be, for even good men will succumb to tales of vast treasure and glory if given time. At first knowledge, disembark them, with such that they shall not seek revenge in spite."

Again, Markus nodded, as, like the first man, this one sat back, with a look of authority on his face. He, too, lifted his tankard for a drink. Markus looked at the third man. This one, Markus had noticed from the start, was different from the other two. Not only was his skin much darker, his hair was covered completely with a rather dirty red scarf tied over it, rather than him wearing a hat with a Captain's ratings like the others. He sat slightly apart from them, never looked at either, or

Sean, or Markus, his eyes shifting around the tavern constantly or cast down at the table.

His tankard handle never left is hand. He was constantly bringing the tankard to his lips, though he did not seem to drink much with any lift, he did drink often. He signaled the barmaid for another tankard and said not a word until the fresh drink was before him and the empty removed.

Markus glanced at the other two men just after the drink was delivered. He saw the barely concealed contempt in the men's eyes. He looked back at the third man when he began to speak, even more softly than the other two. Markus had to shift slightly and lean far forward to hear him. Markus' nose wrinkled slightly due to the odors drifting from the man, and the smell of his foul breath caused by the ale and the man's rotting teeth.

"I know… of things… but they shall cost ye… cost ye much… but you will pay, and be glad for the knowing of what I know."

Markus drew back slightly, more from the smell than the man's words, though he did not like them much, either.

"Now, donna be backing away, mon. Ye be well advised to accept what I have to say." Markus' eyes narrowed even more than the man's, when his narrowed in warning.

Markus kept his eyes on the man, not glancing over to see what expressions Sean and the other two men might have on their faces. He would not have been reassured in the least, had he looked.

"Careful, my man," Markus growled, his Irish brogue much more noticeable than usual.

"Not your man, mon!" replied the man forcefully, his eyes flicking up to meet Markus' for the first time. He dropped them just as quickly, and then scanned the room again, before again looking down at the tankard in his hand.

This time his words were almost a hiss, "If you do not pay, um… five doubloons, you will get nothing from me."

Markus leaned back in the chair. "Then I shall get nothing from you."

The man looked shocked. And then angry again when Markus added, "One doubloon. No more," before the man could speak himself.

The man opened and then closed his mouth several times before speaking. Again, it was a hiss. "Two. Two doubloons. And the information is worth far more than that. You will see. You will see. Without it, you will not last a single sailing."

Markus simply stared at the man for several seconds, and then nodded. "Very well. Let's hear it."

The man sat a bit straighter, but glared at Markus. "Gold first," he said.

Though Markus hesitated a few heartbeats, he pulled out his purse and extracted two gold doubloons, put them on the table, and then slid them over toward the man. Markus' hand had barely left the coins when the man had them and they disappeared somewhere in his dirty clothing.

The man made a motion with his left hand, which immediately raised Markus' awareness, as well as the two other men. All three of them had a hand on a weapon before the appearance of a young man from near the rear door of the tavern.

Once he was closer, Markus relaxed slightly, and released his hold on his cutlass. It was no man. The lad might have been fourteen, but was probably only eleven or twelve.

The third man growled something to the boy that was too low for Markus to hear, but the boy withdrew some parchment from inside his tunic and handed it to Markus.

Markus held it up, looking at the third man. "Canna' write. The boy here writes for me. It's my eyes, you see…"

All three of the others had the same thought. It was not the man's eyes. He was simply illiterate.

Without saying another word, the third man drained his tankard, and stood with some difficulty. The boy followed the hobbling man out through the back door of the tavern. Markus took a close look at the sheets of parchment. The writing was small, but very neat and easily readable. Along with the written pages, were three sheets that had nicely drawn, fairly detailed maps on both sides of the parchment.

The other two men called for another tankard each while Markus studied the parchment. He scanned most of it, then rolled the pages up before putting them inside his jacket.

"I must go," Markus told the other two men and Sean. "And thank you, gentlemen. Good evening." Markus signaled the barmaid, paid for tankards they had consumed so far, and requested another pair for the men. He and Sean left the tavern, shook hands, and Markus headed back to what would be his home for the next many months.

It was only another day and a half before the Irish Rose set sail. And almost half of that was simply waiting for the tide to change. Markus had opened his mouth one last time just before everyone boarded the ship, to plead with Aislinn to stay ashore and head for Boston, but he closed it before even speaking upon seeing the expression on his sister's face and the glint in her eyes. Aislinn and Morgana would be going with him to the Caribbean.

Markus made good use of the time taken to sail south. Some of each day was spent continuing with the crew's training to improve their handling of the ship. Another part of the day was spent using the extensive amount of extra munitions Markus had decided to carry on the gun deck and the top deck, in addition to that stored in the Irish Rose's large magazines.

While he would never have such quantities stored on the decks normally, Markus wanted the extra with which the crew could practice their gunnery. Having proven more than adequate during the sea trials, Markus knew that the better a ship's gunnery was, the more likely it would not have to be used nearly as often, not only because it would take fewer rounds to accomplish what was needed, but as the Irish Rose's reputation grew it was far more likely that many of the prizes that Markus intended to go after would strike their flag and surrender with no more than a shot across their bows.

It was not unknown for merchant ships to surrender upon seeing a ship commanded by a pirate with a powerful reputation to strike and surrender as soon as the pirate hoisted his Pirate flag, indicating his intentions.

With this in mind, the Irish Rose practiced gunnery, sometimes on a set schedule, sometimes when Markus would call for action at unexpected times. It quickly became apparent that not only was Morgana an excellent gunner herself, whether it was her fae senses or not, she also had a knack for imparting the information and skills to others, despite her gender.

Though still a bit recalcitrant about having women on board, much less one training them, the crew, to a man, quickly became to not only accept, but appreciate Morgana's abilities. For shortly after Markus instituted a prize system for the gunnery practice, and every crew that was being trained by, or led by, Morgana, almost always took the prize for the day, every man wanted her to help improve his own performance. Because not only was the winning crew rewarded, individual rewards were given for performance improvements.

And since Hernando, who had been appointed to be in charge of gunnery due to his previous experience in the Spanish Army land artillery, had known Morgana for a long time, made no protest when Morgana took over the job. It was even he that suggested it to Markus. Hernando became her second in command of the guns.

The rowing was not forgotten, either. With much grumbling, which was very rare from the crew, the oars were shipped during the first training chance, and the confusion began.

Markus wondered a few times if the lack of success was more the crew's reluctance to do what was now usually considered equal to being a slave than it was the men's actual inability to master it.

Markus, who was becoming more and more a Ship's Captain and Master, and in general leader of men, did the same as with the gunnery.

A prize system was instituted, with prizes for the rowing crew, which became crews due to the prize system, as well as individual awards for doing specific tasks related to rowing. From mounting the rowing seats to shipping the oars, unshipping them and stowing the oars and seats, and even one-person oar maneuvers to get the ship to turn a specific way.

Where Morgana was highly capable with the ship's armament, when Aislinn remembered something from her schooling lessons in history and began to emulate that particular aspect of rowed vessels in even ancient times, the rowing suddenly became far easier, much more coordinated and therefore very much able to move the ship faster.

All it took was a small drum that she initially borrowed from one of the men, and her sitting somewhat in front of the first set of oars, setting the pace with the beat of that drum. It worked far better than Ricardo's attempts at doing the same thing with his voice.

When the first volunteer crew began getting very nice prizes for their work, enough additional men volunteered to be oarsmen, as well, to form a second full crew, with additional men willing to fill in.

Three sessions of training, including practice switching the rowing crews while under way, and it began to look like Markus had made a very good decision. A couple more and everyone admitted that it definitely was. And since Markus made a point to adjust the division of any bounty for those that would row, it was accepted without further question.

Three times they saw ships on the horizon, on a course and close enough, for the Irish Rose to intercept, but Markus maintained the ship on the plotted course.

One of the things that Markus agonized over, and there were many of them, was whether to use any of the information that third, dark skinned man at the tavern had presented him. It did seem like very useful information, if it was true. And Markus had that gut feeling that it was. His gut feeling had never failed him before. It was akin to Aislinn's fae abilities, but different in ways neither he nor she could explain.

Finally, when the time came to decide on the final destination, Markus went with his gut and the information on the parchment. Markus, Aislinn, Ricardo, and Meyer Olinskie, one of the additional crew that Ricardo had found during the days of the construction of the Irish Rose, each plotted the course toward a small island east of Nassau. Not only for the navigation practice, but as a double check on Markus' own navigation skills, which were still somewhat rough.

The Irish Rose did reach the island, and the tiny cove which cut its shoreline, near the time they had calculated. The island and cove were just as the old seaman had said. There were only a handful of trees on the island, and no wildlife other than some birds and a few small rodents scurrying about between the clumps of grass growing here and there on the sand of the island.

The tiny fresh water spring was right where the parchment said it would be. Markus ordered the Irish Rose's water barrels refilled, again using the task to do some training with the long boats, cargo tackle, and equipment the Irish Rose carried for such missions.

After a day to rest, and correct the few additional minor problems that had come up on the trip, Markus turned the brigantine toward Nassau. He boldly sailed the Irish Rose into the harbor and dropped anchor. Leaving a protesting Aislinn on board, along with Ricardo, First Mate and responsible for the non-sailing crew in charge, Markus had four of the crew row him to the docks, where he headed for one of the contacts listed on the parchments.

It did not take him long to do his business with the man, once he found him, sobered him up, paid him a few pieces of eight, and asked the questions Markus wanted answered.

With the knowledge gained, Markus went back to the Irish Rose, talked to Ricardo and Meyer for a few minutes, and then Aislinn. Meyer, the Second Mate and in charge of the sailing crew, set up a schedule for the crew to go ashore a few men at a time, always with Meyer, Ricardo, or Hernando with the group. Aislinn and Morgana went ashore accompanied by Markus.

While Aislinn and Morgana had gone to wearing either men's clothing, or highly modified women's clothing on board ship for convenience sake, both dressed as proper ladies to go ashore with Markus.

And Markus, though he had always dressed very well, had been persuaded that a Pirate Captain that intended to make a name for himself, for whatever reason, would dress rather more flamboyantly than was his wont. While Aislinn and Morgana had commissioned their clothing to be made while the Irish Rose was under construction, Markus had as well. Reluctantly, he had added several additional pieces of clothing, some of which he wore on this trip into Nassau.

The deep emerald green long frock coat with gold buttons, over a brilliant green shirt of loose, flowing silk, the loose black cotton breeches tucked into polished black over-the-knee leather boots, red silk sash, and the black tri-corner hat with gold stitching atop his long mane of red hair made Markus a striking sight.

More than a bit self-conscious to start with in the clothing he had selected for the excursion, Aislinn delightedly teased him mercilessly, knowing how he felt. Morgana made sure to keep her smile hidden from him as he became red in the face, and redder still once they were ashore. He finally became inured to it and quit responding and his color returned to normal, so Aislinn lost interest and began to examine her surroundings as they entered the town.

The black leather baldric over his right shoulder supporting the scabbard for his cutlass with its highly embellished grip on his left hip, and three flintlock pistols in pouches across his chest added a rather more ominous aspect to Markus' look.

With his clear green, intense eyes; broad shoulders and chest; upright posture; and strong, purposeful stride, Markus drew many eyes, not a few of which were in the heads of women, which turned as often as not to watch him on his way, interest in their eyes.

The interest in the men's eyes that followed him was of a different sort entirely. One that had Aislinn hurrying slightly to stay with Markus, close to his side, and Morgana, a step behind her charge to tense slightly, her fingers itching to draw one of the several weapons concealed variously within her clothing and the bag she carried.

Once Aislinn and Morgana were ensconced in the best accommodations to be had for gentlewomen, Markus left them to make his presence known in the town, much to Aislinn's disgust when he absolutely refused to take her with him.

Morgana, while she would not have minded going with him to get a good look around, was just as adamant as Markus that Aislinn not be going out to any of the places that Markus would undoubtedly be visiting.

Both women did wait up for him. Aislinn, because of her intense curiosity about everything, and what they were doing now in particular. And Morgana, of course, because her mistress was.

It was obvious that the very tired looking Markus was more than a bit disgusted when he stopped at their room and told them he had returned safely, a promise Aislinn had extracted from him before he left.

"What is wrong, Markus?" Aislinn asked, noting his expression.

Markus shook his head. "This is a dirty business, Aislinn. I do not know if I… we… should pursue this course of action or not. The people here… Many of them anyway, though certainly not all, are of the lowest order, with vile demeanors and even more vile thoughts that they express on the merest whim."

"Such as…" Aislinn began to ask him.

"You will never hear them from my lips, my sister. Nor, I hope and pray, will you ever hear them from anyone's lips."

Aislinn began to object, but Markus cut her off. "I will explain further tomorrow. Some of it, anyway, but not tonight. I, as well as you, will need your rest for the morrow. We will be sailing with the noon tide."

"But…" Aislinn began to protest, but fell silent at the weary look in Markus' eyes. She nodded sympathetically and closed the door when Markus stepped back to go to his own room.

The next morning Aislinn noted that Markus still looked tired and troubled. After his half-hearted attempt to get her to stay ashore, he wasted no time getting them back to the Irish Rose.

As soon as they boarded after their return to the ship, Markus conferred with Ricardo and Meyer. Reassured that all the crew were aboard and the Irish Rose was ready to sail, Markus instructed them to get ready to sail with the noon tide, and then come down to his cabin.

Markus busied himself in the Captain's cabin as Aislinn and Morgana got their cabin ready for whatever might come, and then since Aislinn and Morgana had agreed to take charge of the cooking for themselves as well as the crew, they went over the particulars to make sure everything was ready, there as well.

Markus made no objection when Aislinn and Morgana entered his cabin a bit later, and moved out of the way as Markus explained to Ricardo and Meyer what his plan was, given the information he had obtained in Nassau. Aislinn's eyes grew wide as she listened. Things were starting to become very real to her now.

"I do not know just how reliable the information is," Markus told Ricardo and Meyer. "From what I was told in Savannah, the people I talked to here have been reliable in the past. But that does not mean they are now. At least one of them has anger for the Irish for some reason. But the opportunity can't be ignored. If the information is accurate, this should be a very good start to our campaign."

Ricardo simply nodded in agreement. Meyer, on the other hand, had a few questions. The first, "How tight must we control the crew? There are several that have pirated before. With several of the worst of the Captains now in this area. They are more than a bit bloodthirsty. How will we handle prisoners... and such?"

Markus hesitated for a bit before answering.

"We are not savages," Markus said. "We will be humane to the prisoners, but we will be strict with them. As long as they surrender, and agree to my terms, they will be kept fed and watered, until they can be put ashore in a safe place where they will be found without too long of a wait. If any wish to join us, they will be required to sign the Articles, just as every one of us has, and will suffer the consequences if they break that faith.

"And," Markus added quickly, "If we encounter any women at all, they will be treated with respect and courtesy. They will not be touched."

Ricardo and Meyer both nodded. Markus could not tell just exactly how Meyer felt about the situation, whether he agreed with it or not.

"One more thing," Markus said, "There will be no involvement in slavery. At all. We will free any that we might run across. We will not make slaves of any person we capture. Nor profit from any existing slave. That is an absolute, just as it is with women."

Again, Markus could not tell if Meyer agreed or disagreed. He put it out of his mind and went on to other topics.

"Similar question," Meyer said then. "Gunnery. How much damage are we to inflict? Ship wise and crew wise?"

"We will keep it to a minimum. Only what is required to force a surrender."

Meyer nodded again. "And the Navy?"

"We are not at war," Markus replied. "We will avoid all warships whenever possible. We will not engage any naval ships, except those of the Spaniards. We will not seek them out, but if we cannot avoid them, we will defend ourselves, using whatever force we must to make our escape, or to defeat them. If they were to surrender to us, they would be treated the same as any other captives."

Another set of nods and Markus waited for a few moments. There were no more questions. Markus then went into the details of the upcoming voyage, the three men huddled over the charts on the chart table.

Aislinn and Morgana continued to listen in, but were not concerned with the various details of course, speed, winds, tides, and such. They did key in on any details of the ship they were going after. They shared a wide-eyed look when Markus told the men, "She should be a sweet prize. One of the treasure galleons, sailing without escort, trying to beat the weather that is coming.

"It is rumored she will be drawing a deep draft, and will be sluggish and slow. But this Captain is one willing to chance things alone. She is heavily armed, far out gunning us in both size and number of cannon. But there were no indications of just how effective the crew is with the armament. We, on the other hand, have excellent gun crews, and I do believe we will be able to get her to drop her colors fairly quickly."

Meyer did have one more question, just as they were finishing up. "Our colors?"

Markus smiled at that. He looked over at Aislinn and Morgana, and lifted his eyebrows. Aislinn nodded and stood up to go over to one of the trunks secured out of the way in the cabin.

She opened the trunk, and with Morgana's help, removed and held up the pirate flag that they had sewn up. It was the basic black flag often used by pirates, but with some additions, such as a few other Pirate Captains were wont to do.

On each side of the flag, stark against the black cloth, was a long stem, green, curving up from near the bottom of the flag, ending with an elaborate green petal rose. Along the stem were large green thorns, with bright red tips.

Ricardo and Meyer both grinned and gave appreciative nods. And with that, the two left the cabin.

Since it was coming up on noon, when the tide would be going out on which the Irish Rose would sail, Aislinn and Morgana left Markus' cabin and went to prepare a meal for themselves and the crew so they would be fed and able to work through the noon hour as the ship set sail.

Aislinn and Morgana went topside to watch, but, as always, stayed out of the way. Both women, however, studied everything, soaking the knowledge up just as they did with everything they involved themselves with.

With Markus at the wheel, Ricardo and Meyer relaying his orders, the Irish Rose sailed smartly out of the harbor.

CHAPTER FOUR

The weather cooperated with them, and the Irish Rose had smooth sailing to the area where they hoped to find the Spanish Treasure Galleon Nuestra Señora de Esmeralda.

Markus had the Irish Rose sailing a broad zig-zag course northeast of the route that the Esmeralda would most likely take. A lookout was posted high in the ship's rigging at all times, watching for the galleon. With the taller than usual mast for a brigantine that meant the look-out was up very high, giving a very long-range view of the surrounding ocean.

To keep the crew from becoming bored with the slow back-and-forth sailing, Markus instituted some training sessions, as well as some fun-and-games activities.

Most of the men that had worked for Markus had some education, thanks in part to Aislinn's efforts working with the men and their families. Most of the additional crew had very little, if any.

After the initial resistance to being instructed by a woman, again, most of the men took to the lessons willingly. Aislinn, having gone through the process before, made the learning fun for the men.

Markus also taught a few things, as well. Though Aislinn was highly skilled at swordplay, Markus was sure the men would not take to her teaching them the skill, despite accepting her other teachings. Markus did use her as his training partner to demonstrate sword handling techniques.

Which was a bit of an incentive to the men, for they were eager to learn, in order not to be considered less skilled than a woman.

This went on for eight days, before the current lookout shouted "Ship ho! Two points off the starboard bow!"

Markus signaled to Ricardo and he called the crew to prepare for battle. The men dropped what they were doing, in this case, doing another thorough cleaning of the ship, something Markus was adamant about.

In less than three minutes Meyer called out his sailing crew was ready, and Ricardo relayed the word to Markus and also reported his deck and gunnery crews were also ready.

Markus took the helm and steered a course toward the ship, based on the lookout's directions, as Markus could not yet see the ship over the horizon.

With a command from Markus, Meyer had the crew adding more sail. A couple of hours later, the Esmerelda's sails were visible from the deck of the Irish Rose. Apparently, the lookout on the Esmerelda saw the Irish Rose's sails, for more sails suddenly billowed on the other ship.

It was far too late, and far too little. Not only was the Irish Rose faster anyway, but the Esmerelda, as Markus had been told, was riding low in the water from the heavy load she carried. The Galleons were not built for high speed to start with, as they were usually escorted.

Captain Banderos, if he was the captain of the Esmerelda as Markus had been told, was known to be an aggressive captain, and had travelled alone more than once. He was also known to not simply surrender his ship when threatened. He had fought off pirates twice before.

Markus and crew were about to find out, as the Irish Rose rapidly gained on the Esmerelda, despite the full set of sails she was carrying. Irish Rose was fast enough, and maneuverable enough, to not only catch up to the Esmerelda, but to get past her, well out of range of her guns, and turn slightly, lose way, and bring her guns to bear, where the Esmerelda could only respond with her forward chase guns.

And the Esmerelda's chase guns were only nine-pounders, and not the Long-nines like the Irish Rose carried, so did not have the range that of the Irish Rose's twenty-four pounders, or even the eighteen-pounders.

After running up the Irish Rose's colors, the green rose on black flag with thorns dripping red, Markus had the gun crews fire a seven-gun broadside, with three twenty-four pounders and four eighteen pounders from the port side gun deck. With the skill of the crews, all guns except for one of the eighteen-pound guns had the range.

Markus had ordered the broadside as a warning, and the ship had been turned just enough for the shots to land just off the port side of the Esmerelda. It was very obvious that the Irish Rose could do serious damage to the Esmerelda, while staying out of range of her less capable guns.

Even with the advantage the Irish Rose was obviously showing, Captain Banderos' arrogance would not allow him to strike his colors. The nine-pounders forward fired, the rounds falling far short of the Irish Rose.

Markus' expression hardened. He brought the ship about, as the Esmerelda continued to approach, and begin to turn, to bring her heavy guns to bear on the Irish Rose.

This time, as his guns came to bear, the twelves, eighteens, and twenty-fours, Markus' orders were to aim for maximum damage.

Though the twelve-pounders were just in range, they too helped lay waste to the upper decks of the Esmerelda and her rigging. Since Captain Banderos had turned his ship, and it was at one quarter to the Irish Rose broadside, the damage was extensive.

Only three of the Esmerelda's cannon fired, two far too early to bear, and the third far after having passed the proper firing point. When Markus saw the Esmerelda's colors come down he ordered his gun crews to cease fire. Every gun was reloaded and ready when he sailed the Irish Rose toward the Esmerelda.

More than a bit nervous, Markus ordered Aislinn and Morgana below decks as they approached the port side of the Esmerelda. Nothing happened other than an officer of the Esmerelda offering her surrender. It was very obvious the officer was not Captain Banderos,

both from the uniform he wore, and his demeanor. When Markus asked, the officer admitted that both the Captain and First Mate had been killed in the volley. He, himself, had chosen to surrender the ship rather than face the Irish Rose's accurate guns again.

When Markus turned around to order Ricardo to take a crew over to secure the Esmerelda, he saw Aislinn guarding his back, her cutlass drawn. With Morgana doing exactly the same thing for Aislinn, her cutlass out in her right hand and a flintlock pistol in her left.

Markus muttered something, but turned back around to be ready to assist if any of the Spanish decided to disregard the surrender. And with their Captain having chosen to fight, they expected rough treatment, so such a thing was very possible.

The transfer of power went smoothly. With Ricardo's men having the Spanish crew secured, Meyer took a sailing crew across to man the ship.

Despite his orders, Aislinn and Morgana were in full evidence to the Spanish. Despite wearing trousers, it was obvious they were both women, with their fair complexions and long, flowing hair. And it was just as obvious how well they were armed.

The Irish Rose's crew, seeing the Spanish crew's eyes on the two women, and hearing some of the remarks they were making, made it very clear, proudly, just how skilled the women were, and despite that, anything any of the Spaniards might do to endanger or demean the women would be met with harsh consequences at their hands, long before the women could have a chance at them.

The prize crew from the Irish Rose, after securing the Spanish crew below decks of the Esmerelda, began the process of getting the Esmerelda ready to sail again. Though the damage the Irish Rose had inflicted on the Esmerelda looked to be great, there really was not that much to do to get her ready to sail.

Cutting away the damaged rigging and letting it go overboard, clearing the upper decks of the other damage, and Meyer was soon ready to hoist sail. After a last exchange between Markus and Meyer, both ordered their men aloft to set sail.

The Esmerelda had been slow before, and missing so much of her rigging, was now even slower to sail. Markus was in no hurry. With an eye on the weather, Markus decided to sail a wide sweeping course to get back to Nassau.

It was well he did, for deep, dark clouds, with heavy lightning and rain were on the horizon for almost the entire journey. They diverted once to one of the small islands that was visited often. There the Spanish crew were put ashore, with enough supplies to keep them going for long enough to be sure someone found them before they ran out.

As was customary, the Spanish crew members were given the opportunity to join the Irish Rose's crew. Only one did so, rather eagerly it seemed to Markus. The man agreed to and signed the Articles. The rest declined. As they had been well treated, the rest of the crew gave the Irish Rose's crew no trouble.

Just before they reached Nassau, they did have to reduce sail, and steer a course to avoid the storm that had finally intersected their course. It was only half a day before the skies cleared and Markus turned the ships once again to Nassau.

As soon as the two ships were sighted, a dozen small ships and boats came out of the harbor to meet them.

Questions were shouted up at the crews on both ships, but Markus had given instructions that no one was to give any information pertaining to Markus, the Irish Rose, and their operation.

The crews did well, mostly just exchanging insults and inane conversation. Markus was pleased that by the time they were at anchor in the harbor, none of the crew had given anything at all away about what the Esmerelda carried.

With the ships anchored together, and guards out on both, Markus was comfortable enough with the situation to head into Nassau to meet with the man that would most likely buy the Esmerelda.

Aislinn did not press Markus to go with him, knowing the places he would be were no places for her to be. What she did, with Morgana's and Ricardo's help while Markus was gone, was to do an inventory of the Esmerelda's holds. They had been off limits to everyone during the journey, access blocked, so there would be no question about anyone taking anything they were not entitled to receive, based on the agreements in the Articles.

As heavily laden as the Esmerelda was, her cargo was packed and arranged very well, making it relatively easy for the three to locate, identify, and verify everything by eye against the manifest that had been in Captain Banderos' cabin.

With the double checked manifest in hand, Aislinn met with Markus when he returned late that night. He looked extremely tired, Aislinn thought, but not unhappy. When she lifted an expressive eyebrow in question, Markus managed a small smile. "We did well," he said. "A fair price for the ship. Though he does not want any of the cargo we choose not to keep."

Aislinn nodded. "I understand. Here is the manifest. We did a very careful check, verifying everything. It is just as the manifest lists." Aislinn grinned. "There are a few things I would like to claim as my share."

Markus chuckled. "Of course, Little Sister." He was looking at the manifest. Aislinn saw his eyes widen slightly. She was pretty sure she knew what caused it, but said nothing.

When Markus looked up again, she excused herself and headed off to bed, to let Markus get some rest himself. He would be busy the next couple of days, making arrangements for the cargo they would not distribute to the crew and keep for themselves, to be sold to the highest bidder at an auction.

The first thing Markus did the next morning was put quill to paper. He wrote letters to the Spanish authorities in Spain and in Mexico, explaining his actions, and warning them that until Padilla and Chavez were removed from the Lynch estate and restitution made, he would continue to punish Spain in every way he could.

The letters finished, Markus made arrangements on shore for them to get to their destinations. Then, with Aislinn and Morgana accompanying him to do a bit of shopping, Markus confirmed at several places in town that there would indeed be an auction of luxury goods from the Spanish Galleon within a week, and where it would be.

Aislinn did not buy much, and Morgana nothing. They were just simply along to be able to spend some time off the ship, in safe company.

When they returned, and to the great delight of the crew, Markus, with Ricardo and Meyer beside him, gave the tally of the sale of the Esmerelda, the expected sales of the goods they were not keeping, and of the items that were of the type that would be distributed as compensation to the crew as per the Article's listed arrangement.

Several of the crew, the more experienced ones, did look over the manifest and Markus' tally, before agreeing to the distribution. When the final distribution was done early that evening, many very happy members of the crew went ashore. Less happy were the ones that had drawn the lots to stay behind that night, but would be on shore the next night.

Markus carefully packed away the things he took as the Captain's share. He had chosen only minted gold and silver coins and bullion after all the coins had been distributed, for his share.

Aislinn had taken a couple of pieces of jewelry, and several bolts of silk and other cloth that had come from India, by way of Mexico, along with a share of the coinage.

Morgana, took only a bit of the cloth, and the rest in coin and bullion for her share.

Markus had been pleased that the crew had made no objections when the distribution was made, and the women were handed the shares they had chosen.

The transfer of the powder, shot, and other items from the Esmerelda that could be used on the Irish Rose were transferred the next day. After that, the rest of the cargo was unloaded from the Esmerelda, and taken to shore, to get it ready for the auction.

Markus was not too pleased having to stay in Nassau for as long as it wound up taking to get the auction set up for the sale of the Esmerelda's cargo. He was anxious to get back out to sea. Not only was he getting bored himself, but Aislinn was as well, and when Aislinn was bored she was likely to get into trouble.

And though the crew had done very well about not getting too wild in Nassau, Ricardo and Meyer both suggested that things were going to start getting worse if they stayed in the harbor much longer.

Thankfully, the cargo was sold, for considerably more than Markus was expecting, and with several more possible leads, Markus ordered the crew to ready the ship for sailing on the next high tide some seven hours after he had collected the proceeds from the auction.

Only a couple of the crew did not show up when they were supposed to, which was not actually that bad of a loss. Markus had been told that a ship could lose half or more its crew after a successful pay out.

One of those that did not return was the Spaniard that had left the crew of the Esmerelda to join the Irish Rose. Again, Markus was not at all unhappy about that.

Just before the sun set, Markus guided the Irish Rose out of the harbor at Nassau, and had the crew put on full sail, turning the Irish Rose west once they were clear to do so.

Aislinn, Ricardo, and Meyer all questioned Markus' decision to head into the Gulf of Mexico to try and intercept a treasure Galleon close to its departure point. There would be more risk of running into Spanish warships that often cruised near the coast to be available to help the Spanish Army if there was trouble on land getting gold and silver to the ports, and in the ports, before it could be loaded onto the Spanish treasure ships.

And though the Irish Rose could post a lookout far higher than most brigantines, the Spanish Navy had some larger warships in the area that had lookouts high enough to be able to see further than the lookouts on the Irish Rose.

All three were more than willing to follow Markus' leadership and said nothing more when Markus reconfirmed his orders. There was smooth sailing for many days as they did a tacking course, making good progress despite the steady westerly winds.

They saw not a single other ship until they came within several miles of the Mexican coastline. And the first several ships they did see were fishing vessels. Those they left strictly alone, changing course if need be to stay well away from them, never showing their colors.

Then the Spanish Navy saw them. The Spanish frigate was under full sail, headed toward the Irish Rose when the Irish Rose lookout spotted the frigate's sails.

The winds were highly favorable to the Spanish frigate, and despite Markus turning the Irish Rose to try and avoid the ship, even before it was obvious that it was a warship, in order to get to a point where the Irish Rose could get closer safely and find out if it was a treasure ship or not, the frigate began to get closer.

With the frigate intentionally trying to close on the Irish Rose, there was no way to avoid it, and get into a more favorable position to check it out without giving away the fact that the Irish Rose was a pirate ship. And as soon as it became clear that it was, in fact, a Spanish Navy war frigate, Markus decided to try and simply avoid contact.

Despite a valiant effort, there was simply no way to avoid the frigate. The winds just were not suitable for the Irish Rose to be able to escape. After a quick consultation with Aislinn, Ricardo, and Meyer, Markus decided not to go ahead and escape, once the Spanish Frigate was close enough that the Irish Rose could again maneuver effectively in relation to the other ship.

Markus ordered the gun crews to get ready, and the rest of the crew to be ready for a fight with the frigate. The Irish Rose was faster than the frigate and rather more maneuverable, and once she could take advantage of the winds, Markus quickly brought the ship around.

He ordered the colors up, and all the gun crews to fire as they came to bear. The frigate was quartering to the Irish Rose, and only two of her swivel guns were able to return fire before Markus turned the Irish Rose away to avoid getting in a position where the Spanish Frigate could rake them with a broadside.

Again, the expertise of the Irish Rose gunners was the deciding factor in the battle. The first round of cannon fire from the Irish Rose took out enough of the frigate's forward and midship rigging to cripple her. Significant damage was done to the decks, including three of her gun ports, as well.

Markus made the decision to leave the frigate to its fate, and gave orders to set sail westward, again headed for the coast.

When they were nearing the coast, Aislinn, Ricardo, and Meyer could tell that Markus had something on his mind. None of them really thought it had anything to do with the Spanish frigate. Aislinn finally asked him what seemed to be bothering him during one of the meetings they had every evening and morning. It was the morning before they would reach the coast, and then turn south toward the port.

Reluctantly, Markus told the three. "I was just thinking about the possibility of trying to hit one of the mule trains bringing in the gold and silver from the mines, and from the mint to the port. My information indicates that they are scheduled to be travelling close to this coast right now.

"But it would be very risky. I just do not think it is worth the risk. Or even possible."

Meyer shrugged his shoulders, and with the meeting over anyway, went back on deck to attend to business. Ricardo looked thoughtful. "Let me talk to Hernando," he said. Without waiting for a response from Markus, Ricardo left, still with the thoughtful look on his face.

When Markus looked over at Aislinn, almost pleadingly. "Sorry, brother," she said, "If they can come up with a plan, I am all for it." She left his cabin as well, but with a smile on her face, due to Markus' sour expression.

Despite Markus' intention to not even try for the mule train that he was quite sure would be where he had been told it would be, when they arrived in the area, he made a snap decision. Hitting the mule train had been in his mind from the time his source had told him of its existence, but the worry overrode his desire. Markus did not want to lose any of the crew, especially those that had come from Georgia.

They were still out of sight of shore when Ricardo and Hernando approached Markus, who was at the wheel. "Captain, Hernando and I can do it, sir. As long as they are not too far inland."

"Ricardo," Markus said, shaking his head. "It is too risky. And it could delay us too long to catch that galleon in port."

"No, sir, it isn't too risky, and there would be almost no delay," Ricardo replied. He looked over at Hernando, and then turned back to Markus. "Our plan is to take two of the long boats, with just a few of the men that came with us from Georgia.

"We work very well together, and most of us speak the language. We have excellent arms, and are still in very good physical shape, and can move quickly. If you will sail in close enough for us to get the long boats to shore, we will take the mule train, come back to the long boats, and sail toward you. When you take the galleon, sail back toward us, and pick us up."

Ricardo grinned. "We might even get there before you are ready to leave."

"Ricardo…" Markus said, shaking his head.

"They can do it," Aislinn said from beside Markus. She had come up without Markus noticing while Ricardo was speaking.

Markus looked around at her. He sighed. Then nodded. "Very well. We will do it. Prepare the men and the boats."

Ricardo and Hernando hurried off. Aislinn put a hand on Markus' shoulder. "I think this is the best thing," she said softly. "They will be all right. Ricardo and Hernando are good leaders. And our men are good men, skilled at many things. They will persevere, with as little risk as possible. And they want to do this. For themselves. And for you, Markus."

"I know, Aislinn," Markus said. "It is just… I worry…"

"So do I, Markus."

Aislinn turned and hurried off, to do what she and Morgana could to help Ricardo and the men get ready.

It was only a little over two hours before the Irish Rose sails were lowered, and the two long boats dispatched toward the coast, less than fifteen minutes of sail and rowing away.

With a sigh, Markus ordered full sail to take advantage of the freshening winds, and turned south, toward the port, where the galleon should be taking on the treasure load already there.

The winds were with them, so Markus was able to get the Irish Rose near the harbor, staying close to the coast. They saw no one at sea, nor on shore although there was no guarantee that someone ashore had not seen them and reported the sighting.

It did not appear to be so, as on the morning of the day after arriving and hiding overnight in a small cove, when Markus guided the ship from the cove and sailed boldly into the mouth of the harbor, there was no reception party.

There was certainly some curiosity when Markus turned the ship, right in the harbor entrance, starboard side facing the town, and dropped sails and anchors. It was only a few minutes before a boat was readied to leave the dock, a uniformed man in the bow, watching the Irish Rose.

Markus had been waiting for that, and upon seeing the uniformed man signal the oarsmen to lower the oars in preparation to rowing out to the Irish Rose, he quietly gave the order that the crew was waiting for with eagerness. "Hoist the colors," was followed by, "Run out the guns."

It was quite obvious when the uniformed man and his boat crew saw the activity. The uniformed man pitched forward and nearly went overboard when the oarsmen suddenly quit rowing, with oars still in the water, bringing the boat to a sudden stop within just a few feet.

The uniformed man's voice could just barely be heard aboard the Irish Rose as he shouted at his boat crew to begin rowing again, but the crew apparently had other ideas. They rowed, all right, but not toward the Irish Rose.

They turned the boat around smartly, the uniformed man again almost going overboard. He quickly sat down as the men rowed rapidly back to the dock. There, the uniformed man was shouting something at the men when they left the boat, his arms waving, until they ran away.

The uniformed man strode away, obviously angry, cutting a look toward the Irish Rose every so often. Markus turned his attention to the Spanish Galleon. Behind him, Aislinn said softly, "Looks like we got here just in time."

"Yes," Markus replied. He had seen the activity on board the galleon as the Irish Rose sailed in on the tide. Markus was sure the galleon was being readied to sail when the tide turned, in less than three hours.

There was frantic activity aboard the galleon. The bow was pointed toward the harbor entrance, so only their bow chase cannon could bear on the Irish Rose, whereas the Irish Rose starboard guns were bearing on the galleon. And though it was doubtful the Captain and crew of the galleon were aware, but with the rowers ready to open the rowing ports and ship the oars aboard the Irish Rose, which would allow the ship to turn enough to put each gun exactly where Markus wanted it, if the time came, the risk was too great anyway.

Markus was sure that the Spanish captain was well aware that if he tried to hoist the galleon's sails in order to maneuver the ship, Markus would fire upon him.

Another of the Irish Rose's boats was ready to be lowered, and Markus went to it and boarded, along with the crew that would row him toward the galleon.

Staying out of range of a musket shot, Markus lifted his hands and cupped them around his mouth. He shouted in Spanish, "Surrender, or face the Irish Rose's guns! You have thirty minutes to raise and then immediately lower your colors."

Markus did not wait for a reply, though someone was shouting back at him. He ignored the threats as the boat was rowed back to the Irish Rose.

Morgana, as instructed, was watching the spare hourglass. She had turned the glass when Markus had said thirty minutes. When the sand piles were equal, it would be thirty minutes.

Aislinn told Markus that a boat had appeared from behind the galleon, headed for shore moments after Markus had made his demand. "Consulting with the garrison commander, I am sure," Markus replied. He did not even glance at the galleon or the shore.

He ordered the gun crews, rowers and the sailors standing ready to hoist sail to get something to eat, one fourth of them at a time. Aislinn looked exasperated when Markus looked over at her. When one eyebrow arched, she said something under her breath and turned to hurry away.

Markus was watching the hourglass, his back to the galleon and shore. A look at Morgana had her hurrying after Aislinn to get the men fed.

It did not take long for all the men to eat and return to their stations. When Markus told Aislinn and Morgana he was going down to eat in his cabin both looked at the hourglass, and then at him, and then back to the hourglass, their mouths falling open. There was less than fifteen minutes remaining.

Aislinn sputtered a bit, but managed not to say anything, glaring at her brother's back as he went below. She turned to look at Morgana, but Morgana again had her eyes on the hourglass.

Looking back at the shore, and then the galleon, she saw men lined up on the shore and along the galleon's railings. The galleon's boat was being rowed back to the ship, moving quickly.

Aislinn was about to go fetch Markus when he came back up. He was, Aislinn saw in amazement, eating a piece of the chicken she and Morgana had prepared. Still eating, Markus strolled over to the railing and looked at the ship.

Turning his head, he looked at the hourglass. Turning back to the galleon, he raised his right hand. Aislinn and Morgana looked at each other, and then back at Markus. Neither knew what the raised hand meant. It was not a signal. At least they were not aware of it being one. And the Irish Rose's crew did not do anything.

The only activity was the sudden raising of the galleon's flag. Aislinn took a breath and held it, but only for a second. For the galleon's colors came right back down. Her breath whooshed out and she relaxed.

Markus gave quiet orders, and the Irish Rose began to maneuver toward the galleon, under power of the oars, though the crew was ready to unfurl sails at Markus' orders. The boarding crew was ready. Morgana handed Markus the rest of his weapons, and lifted her own, her eyes flicking from Aislinn, to keep an eye on her, and back to the galleon, looking for dangers to her mistress.

As the Irish Rose got closer to the galleon, Aislinn drew her sword, and touched first one and then the other of her pistols, without looking at them, her eyes, too, on the galleon, looking for dangers to her brother.

When the ships were almost touching, two of the Irish Rose crew secured grappling hooks to the galleon. The galleon was taller, of course, so the boarding ramps were lowered so Markus and the rest of the boarding crew could clamber up them to the open decks of the galleon.

The Spanish captain of the galleon, a severe looking man to start with, now looking extremely angry, his eyes shooting daggers at Markus when Markus walked up to him.

More than a bit reluctantly, the Captain handed over his sword, though he hesitated just slightly as he drew it. With Markus' eyes on him, and his sword at the ready, the Captain did not try anything.

Only a few words were exchanged, Markus having trained the Irish Rose crew to not engage in wordplay with any captives. Many of them were more than ready to fight with a Spaniard, as the Spanish crew began spewing invectives at them after realizing there would be no punishment for it.

It was a grueling four hours, as the sun rose higher in the sky. Markus thought about having the Spanish crew help with moving the goods, but decided against it. Aislinn, with Morgana right with her, was the one to go below and decide what would be taken.

Markus had no intention of taking long enough to take everything, though Aislinn insisted on staying long enough to get everything she thought valuable enough to take the risk.

Finally, much to Markus' relief, she came up from below, carrying a small chest herself, and Morgana carrying a rather larger one, her eyes darting, not liking not having a weapon in her hand.

"That is the last of it worth taking," Aislinn told Markus in Gaelic. And then added, also in Gaelic, "The charges are set and burning."

Markus nodded, and after Aislinn and Morgana were safely back on the Irish Rose, he, after pulling the letter he had penned earlier from his coat, tossed it onto the deck, and along with the men guarding the Spanish crew, backed away, and then turned and ran down the boarding planks.

The sails were already unfurling on the Irish Rose, as planned, as the boarding planks were lifted. Morgana and Aislinn were below, as instructed, which surprised Markus as the Irish Rose began to pull away from the galleon.

Markus heard a shot and felt the hot bite of a bullet passing through his left thigh. He heard another shot as his leg buckled and he went down on the deck, and then only the sounds of the ship's rigging, the wind, and the rush of water as the Irish Rose sailed out of the harbor.

At least until the muffled sounds of two gunpowder charges came, signaling the end of the galleon, as tons of water poured into her through the large holes in the hull below the waterline that the charges had opened.

Aislinn ran over to Markus, handing her expended pistol to Morgana. She dropped to her knees, taking stock of the wound in Markus' thigh.

Morgana disappeared, but only long enough to fetch Aislinn's doctoring kit. Aislinn soon had both the entrance and exit wounds covered, with a tight bandage holding them in place.

At a motion from her hand, four sailors rushed forward and carried a protesting Markus down to the spot Aislinn had made her medical area.

When Markus protested that he needed to be back on deck, Aislinn gave him a look that shut him up for a moment. The poke, or whatever she also did that shot a pain through his thigh, helped him make that decision.

He lay back, and let her work on his thigh, lamenting the ruining of a good pair of trousers when she cut them off his leg. With Morgana's help, Aislinn efficiently treated the wounds, using a mix of Irish, Spanish, and American Native medical methods.

Markus finally fell asleep just after Aislinn finished up. She and Morgana cleaned themselves and the area up, changed clothes, and went back up on deck. Meyer had the crew making sail back up along the coast. It was somewhat slow, as they were having to tack often as the winds were from the northeast at the moment.

When Aislinn confirmed that all was well, she went back below to keep an eye on Markus. Morgana took care of preparing food for the crew and everything else that needed doing below decks.

The light was fading when Markus woke up. Aislinn heard Markus groan slightly when he woke. Aislinn fussed over him for a few seconds, feeling his forehead for a fever, and the bandages on the front and the rear of his thigh.

Hiding her smile at his grouchiness, she called for Morgana to help her when Markus insisted on getting up. Markus laid back, deciding that it was probably a good idea to have a bit of help to get up and go on deck.

Though he managed to suppress most of his groans, he did make a few as Aislinn and Morgana assisted him up the ladderway to the open deck. It was a timely move, for Meyer was lowering the sails, losing way quickly.

Markus, Aislinn, and Morgana turned their eyes in the direction Meyer was looking. They saw the sails of the Irish Rose's long boats in the distance. Markus hurried over to the rail, Aislinn and Morgana staying close to him in case he had trouble.

As soon as they were close enough, the crews began to shout back and forth. From the sound of the long boat crews, they had been successful in their quest. Ricardo and Hernando both had large grins on their faces when they stepped out of the long boats after they had been lifted aboard.

Ricardo stepped aside and swept an arm toward his long boat. The crews were eagerly transferring sacks, crates, and chests from the long boats to the decks, before they would be taken below and secured.

"We were very lucky," Ricardo was telling Markus and Aislinn as Hernando and Meyer supervised, with Morgana's help, the movement of the items. "This was the largest treasure train they have ever run, the train master told me."

Ricardo grinned again. "A couple of the soldiers attempted some resistance, but threw down their weapons almost immediately when they saw how many of us there were, and how well we were armed. Even the Spaniard in charge did not put up any resistance. Though he was an arrogant something.

"Only the Spaniard, two of the twelve soldiers, the train master, and his second did not take off when we gave them the chance to leave. Most of them were natives and being forced to work and glad to be freed.

"In addition to the regular collection of treasure the Spaniards usually take from wherever they can, there was a huge quantity of gold and silver coins from the sale of goods to the Americans along the border. And contributions to several of the Spanish churches were being shipped back. It was a tremendously valuable mule train."

"No one hurt?" Markus asked.

"No," replied Ricardo. "None of us were, at all. Only a couple of the soldiers wound up with some bruises, and those were from the Indians that attacked them before they took off. The ones that had mistreated the Indians the most, it looked like."

Markus nodded. "You did well, Ricardo. And Hernando and the men. It was good that you talked me into it. You will be rewarded."

"And how did it go with the Irish Rose?" Ricardo asked.

"It went well," Markus replied.

Aislinn rolled her eyes, and looked down at Markus' bandaged leg.

"Well, fairly well," Markus said. "I did get shot."

Ricardo managed not to laugh at the very different looks on Markus' and Aislinn's faces.

"They were fully loaded," Markus continued, ignoring the look on both Ricardo's and Aislinn's faces. "Well worth the trip. As long as we wind up getting away." Markus glanced up at the Irish Rose's sails as they once again were unfurled and filled with wind, under Meyer's direction.

When Markus grimaced as he turned around, Aislinn insisted he go below to rest. When she moved to help him, Ricardo stepped forward. "I'll lend a hand, if you want to get things ready for him," he said.

Aislinn nodded and hurried away. Markus shot Ricardo a glance. "What?" he asked.

"Well, Sir," Ricardo said, putting Markus' arm over his shoulder to support him, "I may have overstepped my bounds, but just as we left the ambush site, I gave the Spaniard a letter. One similar to the ones you have been giving the ship's captains. Pretty much identifying ourselves and giving the reasons why we are doing what we are doing. Based on a couple of our conversations over the past months."

"I see," Markus said, limping along, his eyes on the deck to avoid stumbling. He did cut a glance over to Ricardo just before turning to back down the ladder to below decks. "And it was as we talked about?"

"Yes, Sir. About Chavez and Padilla, and what they have done."

"Good work, Ricardo. I should have thought to send a letter with you. You are a good friend as well as an excellent and loyal employee."

"Thank you, Sir. We do our best." Ricardo helped Aislinn get Markus into his bed in the Captain's cabin, and then turned and left.

"Wake me if I am needed," Markus told Aislinn, suddenly feeling ready for more sleep.

"Of course," Aislinn replied, knowing only in the most dire of circumstances would she wake him.

Markus did not awaken until early the next morning. He started to rise to get off the bed, but a sharp pain in his thigh drew a loud gasp from him as he lay back. Aislinn was in the cabin moments later.

"Are you all right?" she asked, going to the bed and placing her hand on his forehead to check for fever.

"Were you waiting outside my cabin?" he asked.

"No, Markus. I was coming to wake you. I knew you would want to be up and about."

"What time is it?" he asked, suddenly looking toward the windows at the stern of the ship. He could see bright blue sky.

"Nearly ten," Aislinn replied, not meeting his eyes. She occupied herself with minor things as Markus gaped at her. "Ten! I should have been on deck hours ago! Why didn't you wake me? Or have Ricardo or Meyers come down to do so."

"They both understand you need rest. Everything has been fine. But I know you want to check on things yourself. Once you have been up, and come back down, I will redress your wounds. I will get Morgana to help me get you up on deck.

"But for now, I will help you get out of bed, and then go set up things to redo the dressings while you get ready to go up on deck."

Markus wanted to protest and do things on his own, but knowing that his sister did not mind helping him and that he was better off accepting it, he acquiesced without further argument.

Aislinn supported his shoulders as he sat up, and then steadied him when he stood. She held on for a few moments as Markus made sure he was steady on his feet. When Aislinn was satisfied that he was, she left Markus to do what he needed to do.

A few minutes later, a pale faced Markus sat at the chart table when Aislinn and Morgana stepped into the room after Aislinn had peeked in first to see if he was ready. Leaning on Morgana more than he wished he needed to, Markus went up onto deck.

The hands cheered him and Meyers came over to salute him and then shake his hand. Meyers efficiently explained what he had been doing, with Ricardo's consultation and suggestions.

They were headed east again, this time with friendly winds allowing them to make good time. Markus turned when Ricardo approached listening quietly as Ricardo updated him on several more things, then went into a bit more detailed explanation of his efforts and his crew's during the raid, as well as what they had been up to the last several hours.

Markus was more than satisfied with the situation. To the point where it even annoyed him a bit that everything was going as smoothly without him as it did when he was present.

Pleased, yet somewhat restless, Markus allowed Morgana and Aislinn to take him back to his cabin. He opened his mouth several times to speak as Aislinn tended his wounds again, but closed it each time, thinking that neither Aislinn nor Morgana needed any additional work responsibilities heaped onto them.

After Aislinn tied the last knot in the bandage to hold it in place, she handed the extra items to Morgana, who left, leaving the Captain and Aislinn to have some privacy. She washed her hands, and then turned to look at Markus as she dried them. "What is it, Markus? What is it you want to say, but keep stopping before you say anything at all?"

Markus shook his head as he limped back to his cabin with Aislinn's help. "I do not want to put any more load on you and Morgana, Aislinn. You two do enough, already."

"Markus, we have enough time to do something else. It can't be anything too bad. There just isn't that much to do that isn't being done."

"Well… I am just curious about the treasure…"

"Oh!" Aislinn replied, helping him onto his bed. "I forgot all about that! I intended to inventory everything. I will get that done shortly. For the moment, you get some rest. Morgana will bring in something for you to eat in a little while."

Feeling much stronger that evening after having eaten another filling meal at Aislinn's insistence, passed on through Morgana, since Aislinn had not been to see him since that morning.

Markus was on deck, enjoying the sea air as the Irish Rose made speed to the north east. He made no effort to reassume command of the ship, with Ricardo, Meyer, and Hernando obviously handling everything quite well as First, Second, and Third mates.

He heard a slight shuffle sound and turned to find Aislinn almost to him. She looked tired, but very pleased. "I have the inventory," she said, leaning against the railing and looking out into the darkness. "It is even better than I first thought. Much better. I think that someone is swindling the Spanish government. There are some things that are marked as being one thing, but are something else entirely.

"Like some household goods that turned out to be mostly gold objects, and simply gold coins."

"Hm…" Markus said thoughtfully. "I was told that the Galleon was to carry a few government officials and church clerics that were returning to Spain. I was a bit surprised that they would take up space in a Galleon for them and their personal goods, rather than more treasure."

Markus turned to look at Aislinn. "I think you are probably correct, having discovered those things. Someone made arrangements for what they assumed would be the safest way to get their ill-gotten gains home."

Aislinn heard the humor in Markus' voice when he added, "Their loss, our gain."

As Aislinn accompanied Markus back below, he asked one last thing, "What do you think the entire load is worth?"

When she told him he let out a low whistle. Markus trusted Aislinn's evaluation. She had always been very good with such things, and had only honed her skills at the farm, and now with the treasure accounting.

With the favorable winds, it did not take long for the Irish Rose to reach Nassau again. Only one sighting of a possible warship was made, and it was on the distant horizon when first sighted. It disappeared just a few minutes later as the Irish Rose continued her fast pace toward Nassau.

They did see several ships as they neared the islands, but all were the basic merchant ships that plied the area, moving commercial goods back and forth, and though watched carefully, were no threat to the Irish Rose.

When they dropped anchor in Nassau harbor, several boats headed toward her, looking to sell supplies, provide various services for the ship and the crew, or simply begging for a hand out.

The crew was well trained to deal with them, and Markus was able to get to shore without any problems. He did take Ricardo with him this time, since he was still not back to full fighting form from the gunshot, though Aislinn's treatments had prevented any infection and the wounds were healing nicely.

Ricardo, as always, kept a low profile, making sure Markus was safe as he did his business. After four stops, with the last three of them requiring long walks, rather than being able to ride a horse or get any type of wheeled transport, Ricardo insisted that they stop for a while so Markus could rest his leg.

It did not take much for Markus to agree. He was tired and hurting, and knew he might not be as effective as needed if set upon on the way back to the ship. Stopping in one of the more reputable taverns in the city, Markus gratefully sat down at a table, his back to the wall.

Markus leaned back, letting Ricardo get their draughts. There was a bit of a commotion at one of the tables three over from his, much nearer the bar. When it drew Markus' attention he looked over. Suddenly he slid from the chair and strode as forcefully as he could toward that table.

Despite the injury, Markus was a rather imposing sight, his limp hardly detectible. "Remove your hands from the Lady," Markus ordered. His voice, though low, was strong and definitely carried a threat.

The man holding the struggling bar maid on his lap barked a laugh. "Lady? This ain't here's no lady! This wench has been taunting me since I came in. Just getting my due."

"Release her," Markus said, again with a low voice. The threat was stronger this time, and the words were as much growled as spoken.

The man finally took a good look at Markus. When he saw Markus' expression, and his hand resting on his hip near his cutlass, the man shoved the woman from his lap, leaped up with a roar and began to draw a pistol.

As others scrambled away, Markus did not draw his cutlass, but stepped forward, his left hand going to the man's chest. He was a bit off balance anyway, getting up from the chair, and when Markus gave him a hard shove in his chest, the man when flying backwards.

The pistol that had cleared his belt went flying from his hand, landing near the door of the tavern. When it hit the floor it fired, sending it spinning and the ball slammed into the door frame right at floor level.

Markus could tell that Ricardo was right behind him, so did not worry about someone coming from behind. He concentrated on the downed man. What he did not see until too late was the woman approaching him. She slapped him once, but Markus caught her wrist when the second slap got close.

"I could have handled it," she hissed, her lips inches from his face. "I will lose my job for this, you oaf!" Again, she tried to free her wrist, with the obvious intention of slapping him again. If not worse.

Markus had the presence of mind to shift slightly, so her rising knee would graze his thigh, rather than reach its intended target. Unfortunately, it was his wounded thigh, and the impact send daggers of pain all through it.

The woman's eyes were on his when he winced and groaned slightly at the pain. Her eyes widened slightly, and she quit struggling to get her wrist loose. When Markus' eyes went from her face to something else, she glanced that way, as well.

Markus released her wrist, and his eyes still on the man that approached them, murder in his eyes, said, "Get her out of here Ricardo. I will deal with this lout."

Ricardo really did not want to leave his Captain, more friend than anything, but he did not want to face Markus if he did not do as asked. He got a good grip on the woman, and, like Markus, made sure nothing too vulnerable was exposed to her wrath, and got her out of the tavern.

Though he could not see what happened, Ricardo could hear it and delighted in telling the story for years to anyone interested. Markus ordered the man to stop, but it was obvious he did not.

Since the man had lost his pistol and had no sword, Markus released his hold on the hilt of his cutlass, and with a swift move he had learned from some of the Indians around the Georgia farm, crouched slightly, braced himself, and when the man reached him, grabbed one arm, pivoted, and flipped the man over his shoulder.

Landing hard, the man slid into the bar and simply stayed there, trying to catch his breath. Markus pulled a coin from his waist purse and tossed it to the bar keep before turning on his heel and striding from the tavern, his head high, his stride long, despite the pain he was feeling in his thigh.

Markus stopped in front of the woman, now standing still staring at him. Ricardo had loosened his hold on the woman, and now released her completely to step away.

"Why?" the woman asked Markus. "Why? I have nothing now. Nothing. What am I going to do?"

Markus stared at the woman, stunned. "You were being…"

"I would have dealt with it," she managed to get out, as she obviously attempted to hold back tears.

"I…" Markus stuttered. He straightened. "Very well," Markus said firmly. "Gather your things. We shall find you other employment."

Just as Ricardo shouted, something hit Markus in the back. When he spun around another woman was standing in the door of the tavern, shouting something in a language Markus could not understand, and shaking her hand at the former bar maid.

Markus looked down at what had hit him in the back. It was a bundle of clothing. A very small bundle of clothing, he noted. When he looked back at the bar maid, he saw the sad acceptance in her eyes. She stepped forward, bent over, and picked up the pathetic bundle. When she turned to simply walk away, Markus reached out and touched her shoulder.

"Wait. Please. I am sorry. I just…" Markus closed his eyes and shook his head. When he opened them, the woman was looking up to his face.

"I will make this right," he told her. "I will. I promise. Just come with me back to my ship. We can decide what to do…"

When disgust colored her eyes, Markus winced.

"No. No. Not that. My sister and her attendant are on board. You will be perfectly safe." Markus started. "Unless… Unless you have a husband… Some family… Someone to take you in?"

The woman shook her head. "I will find… something…" she said, almost too softly for Markus to hear as she turned around again and took another step.

Markus looked to Ricardo for help, but Ricardo had the look on his face that said, "I did not start this. It is your responsibility."

"Ricardo," Markus suddenly said, "Run to the ship. Bring Aislinn and Morgana to shore. Hurry."

Markus looked back at the woman and began to walk after her hurriedly. Ricardo was already well on his way to the docks by the time Markus caught up with the woman.

This time he did not touch her, but moved past, walking backwards as he pleaded with her. "Please. I truly am sorry. I did not think about what it would mean. I did not want you to lose your job! I just wanted to protect you!" Markus knew he was pleading like a little child, but he did not care. There was something about this woman that touched him. About her situation, he insisted in his mind.

She lifted her eyes to his again. "Why?" she asked him, eyes searching his face, mostly his eyes.

"I… I… I don't know," he said softly. "I always protect women. It is the way I was raised. And it is just right. And you are…" his words faded as he looked at the vulnerability in her eyes.

"I just couldn't stand to see you treated that way…" he finally added, still softly. "Will you please let me make this up to you? I do know it is my fault. You should not be punished for my actions."

The woman slowed to a stop and continued to just look at Markus' face when he stopped as well. He saw the confusion and uncertainty in her face. "I don't know," she finally said, her eyes dropping. "I don't know what to do. That was my last hope…"

"No," Markus insisted. He put his hands on her shoulders, though very gently. "It is not your last hope. There is always hope. My sister…"

That was as far as he got. A nearly out of breath Aislinn, and a less so Morgana were suddenly there, with Ricardo beside them. As small as she was, Aislinn moved between Markus and the woman. She took the woman's hands in hers. As the two looked at one another, that way that Aislinn had that sometimes scared Markus just a little, seemed to calm the woman more, without a word being said.

Markus saw the woman's shoulders, and then the rest of her relax, while Aislinn held her hands and looked into her eyes. Then Aislinn began to say soothing words that Markus could not really make out. Turning, Aislinn began to lead the woman toward the docks.

Morgana was on the woman's other side, gently taking the woman's small bundle from her, lending her presence to Aislinn's to provide a safe haven for the woman. Markus and Ricardo shared a glance, and then followed silently behind.

Only when they reached the docks did Markus and Ricardo move forward, to get the long boat ready for the three women to board. There was only a tiny hesitation in the woman before she allowed herself to be helped into the long boat.

CHAPTER FIVE

Once aboard the Irish Rose, Markus did not see the woman again until they were again well out to sea, four days later. The goods had been converted into coin, provisions and information acquired, then Markus had headed them out toward another good possibility for taking another prize ship.

This one was not a Spanish Galleon from Mexico. Instead it was one of the Spanish ships that made the loop from Spain to Asia and China, and back, coming around the southern tip of Africa, with precious cargos from the far east and Africa, bound for Europe.

Markus had talked things over with Ricardo, Meyer, and Aislinn. He did not completely trust his source for the information. Even suspected that it might be a trap. The others agreed that since they were aware of the possibility it was worth the risk.

So eastward they sailed, headed for an island off the west coast of Africa that was often used as a scheduled stop for ships on that loop. It was over a week before Markus finally saw the woman again, whose name was Elisabeth.

Aislinn had filled him in on her story. She was the English born wife of a Spanish official sent to Mexico to serve a term in one of the remote areas, but their transport ship had been hit by pirates, and her husband and the crew killed. Elisabeth, being the wife of a Spanish official was held for ransom.

Though unlikely any would be forthcoming, the pirate captain held her unmolested, with the intention of selling her if the Spanish government did not buy her freedom.

Shortly after arriving in Nassau, the Captain was killed in a fight in the very bar where she had been working when Markus ran across her. Since there was really no one else that knew the true situation, as the captain had kept her hidden away and locked up, and his crew had dispersed until he called for them to assemble again, Elisabeth just walked away from the tiny villa the captain was renting.

With nothing to her name, except the one small trunk of clothes she had been allowed to bring, Elisabeth, practical Englishwoman that she was, sought out work. It had been difficult, and she had to abandon the trunk at one point, but found the job at the tavern two weeks after gaining her freedom.

It was difficult, to say the least, working there and living in a tiny, dirty room cobbled onto the back of the tavern, next to the house in which the owners lived. And since she was beautiful, which she tried to hide all the time, the owner's wife hated her, fearful her husband would prefer Elisabeth to her.

The last thing that Aislinn had done before the Irish Rose sailed, with Ricardo escorting her as Morgana stayed with Elisabeth on the ship, was to go ashore and shop for Elisabeth.

Seeing her come on deck, Markus at first thought it was Aislinn he was seeing. He quickly realized it could not be Aislinn, for the woman was much taller than his sister, though rather shorter than Morgana.

It hit Markus that it was Elisabeth. In her new clothes rather than the near rags which she had been wearing at the tavern. He almost lost his breath at the sight. He knew she was pretty. He had seen that even in the clothing she had worn, and the patina of dirt on her at the time she came on board. Now, bathed and dressed the way she was, Elisabeth was beyond beautiful.

He knew he was staring, but could not seem to look away from Elisabeth. At least not until Aislinn came up to him and poked him in the side. He started, looked over at Aislinn, and then hurriedly put his eyes on the sails, and then the rest of the ship, before looking back at Aislinn.

She was grinning at him. "You're blushing, brother."

"No, I am not," Markus said firmly, keeping his eyes away from Elisabeth. With difficulty, which he hoped Aislinn was not noticing.

Of course, she was. Aislinn looked over and watched as Morgana pointed out things on the ship to Elisabeth. "She is a beautiful woman," Aislinn said, the humor obvious in her voice to Markus.

"I suppose," Markus replied, just barely keeping his gaze from the woman under discussion.

Moving around so she could see Markus better, still see Elisabeth, and not interfere with Markus' handling of the ship's wheel and keeping track of the sails.

"You suppose? I guess she is not as pretty as Lady Melissa…"

Markus cut his eyes to Aislinn quickly. "She is far more beautiful than that…"

Aislinn laughed at Markus' protestation. "I see. You did notice. And that is very high praise. I always thought Lady Melissa was quite beautiful. And she certainly did have eyes for you."

"She is a witch," Markus growled. "I never had the slightest interest in her. And you know it." He glanced as his sister again and frowned at the smile on her face.

"Oh, I know. But I think that is not the case with our Elisabeth."

"She is not our Elisabeth," Markus said forcefully. "She is her own woman, quite capable of handling her own affairs, I am sure. She would have to be, to have survived what she has."

Aislinn's hand went to Markus' arm. "I know Markus. I just wanted to get you to admit you have noticed her."

Markus' eyes did finally did go to Elisabeth again. And she happened to be looking right at him when he did. Their eyes locked, and it was Markus that diverted his gaze first.

When Aislinn touched his arm again, he looked down at her. Softly, she said, "She is grateful, Markus. I know that at first, she was angry with you. But, no longer. Elisabeth is a strong woman, but that situation was going to break her. And she knew it."

His eyes still on Aislinn, Markus also spoke softly. "With that the case, make sure she does not focus that gratitude on me. I would not be thinking she owes me in any way."

A quick sideways glance and Markus put his eyes back on Aislinn. "It would not be fair to her… She deserves the best, going through what she did. Don't let her fall for a pirate in mistaken gratitude. And do not let her do anything that could cause her to be accused of piracy when we drop her off."

Aislinn studied her brother for another moment. "Yes. Of course, Markus. I will see to it." She saw the relief in his eyes, but also a flash of disappointment before it was gone, as well. Markus was back to being a Pirate Captain.

When Morgana brought Elisabeth over to the wheel, as the last part of her tour, Aislinn watched as Markus made Elisabeth as comfortable with him as he could. He answered her questions politely, providing her with more information about the ship and its capabilities.

Markus was polite, but reserved. Aislinn finally smiled again when she saw the change in him as Elisabeth turned away, to go with Morgana to help prepare the crew's meal. And a very similar change in Elisabeth, when she thought Markus was not looking at her. "Well, well, well," Aislinn thought.

They were in no hurry, as the ship they were interested in was not due to be at the way point in the islands for several days. Markus kept the Irish Rose at a moderate speed, taking advantage of the winds when they were favorable, but not fighting them too hard when they were not.

They were rather idyllic days on the open ocean for most of the voyage. That began to change, rather rapidly, when they approached the group of islands west of Africa's huge bulge. They passed through two moderate storm systems with very little trouble as they came off the African landmass, but the third was much larger and violent.

Meyer told Markus and Ricardo that the third storm would be a bad one. The other experienced sailors echoed his words. Even Markus and Aislinn were sensing the worsening weather, despite the clear skies and calm ocean at the moment.

With the hope of avoiding the worst of the approaching storm, and intercepting the Spanish ship sooner than they were planning, Markus turned the Irish Rose south, just keeping the coastline of Africa in view.

As it turned out, the distrust of the source of information about the ship proved justified. They found the ship a day after they began their southern course. The large merchantman was sailing under greatly reduced canvas, those aboard also aware of a major storm to their north.

And because of it, the British ship that was shadowing the Spanish one was keeping close, not wanting to get separated if they did run into the storm. There was certainly no real cooperation between the two ships, as England and Spain were still not on friendly terms. Since the British warship had made no move to attack, and the Spanish Captain was worried about pirates, he decided to maintain the course, and hope for the best.

The Spanish Captain did get the best, in the form of the Irish Rose, under Markus' command. And the British Captain got his wish, in the same form. His sole purpose was to capture any pirates that fell for the story they had planted. The fact that it was the Irish Rose was simply a plus in his eyes. Irish Red, Gentleman Pirate of the Caribbean would soon be his captive, bound for the gallows.

When the lookout on the Irish Rose spotted the two ships, Aislinn, Markus, Meyer, and Ricardo held a quick meeting. They had already discussed various options for the different situations they might find themselves in on the trip.

They modified the plan they had come up with earlier that would include the British warship being at hand, to take into account the weather as it was developing.

Meyer was none too happy with the plan, but Ricardo and Aislinn both agreed with Markus that though daring, it would work, with minimum risk from the Spanish ship or the British warship.

The key to it was that the British ship was on the landward side of the Spanish ship, and the Irish Rose was on the ocean side. The second factor that would help the plan work was that the winds were strong westerlies, which greatly favored the Irish Rose on her full canvas run toward the Spanish ship.

Markus gave the quiet order to ready the ship for battle. The crews jumped to, and soon the Irish Rose was ready. When it had become obvious to both the Spanish captain and the captain of the British warship that the Irish Rose was actually going to attack the Spanish ship despite the British being so near, the British captain ordered all sails raised and began the attempt to come up with the Spanish ship in time to protect it and disable the Irish Rose.

Though the Spanish captain first kept enough sail up to provide control, as the Irish Rose bore down on them very quickly, and the British ship was having to tack repeatedly to try to come up to them from the position they had maintained well behind, he turned the ship and put on sail intending to run to the British ship for protection.

Markus had timed it very well, indeed. They were upon the Spanish ship, now with its stern to them, and Markus ordered the as-you-bear broadside with all the starboard guns. Though the Spanish ship did get off two shots from her stern chaser guns, they did not even come close. And the gunners on the Irish Rose, with Morgana providing the inspiration, laid waste to the Spanish ship's masts and rigging.

Instead of pressing home the attack, Markus shifted course slightly and headed directly toward the coast of Africa. Assuming the pirate captain had come to his senses, or his crew had mutinied and taken over the ship, to sail away since facing the British warship would have likely been suicide, or so they thought, the British captain made the decision to leave the Spanish ship to her own devices and changed course to go after the Irish Rose with full canvas on now.

The Irish Rose was exceptionally fast, just as Markus knew. And though the British Frigate was fast, as well, it was not fast enough to come up on the Irish Rose under full sail running before the wind.

Also, since the Irish Rose was very shallow draft for a craft of her size, she was able to sail into places the British ship could not. At least not successfully.

Several of the crew of the Irish Rose thought Markus mad when he ordered reduced sails and let the British warship begin to close on them as they got closer to the coast.

It became very obvious however, to both the crew of the Irish Rose, and the Captain and crew of the British warship, that while the British ship was much closer now, it would not be getting any closer. At least not under its own sail.

Markus had obtained every map and chart he had been able to acquire from the time he had decided to become a pirate. And he had a very good one of that very stretch of coastline. One that showed the many shallows in the coastal waters. Some rather far out from the shore in places.

It was one of those places that Markus had guided the Irish Rose. Since it did not look all that much different from other brigantines, the British captain had no idea of how shallow the water could be and the Irish Rose still sail on it.

What the Captain did know was the draft of his own vessel. And when it ran aground travelling at the fastest speed it could make, he realized that the draft was far more than the depth of the water that the Irish Rose had led it over.

All but one mast snapped at the deck line, and the other up several feet. All did go down, ripping rigging away, causing the sails to billow down, covering all of the forward three quarters of the ship.

The Irish Rose was already turning, heading back out to sea, though it was at a much slower pace as they had to fight the winds that were still from the west. The

Irish Rose was a good sailor with a good crew, and they made the best speed that was possible.

It was still three hours before sunset when Markus had the crew lower the sails and they let the Irish Rose lose way, standing off some distance from the stern of the Spanish ship. The Irish Rose's gun ports were open, and her guns all run out. When Markus asked for the captain to lower the Spanish ship's colors, he did so without hesitation.

It took the rest of the evening before sunset to transfer everything Aislinn wanted from the Spanish ship to the Irish Rose. Markus also ordered all the stores the Irish Rose could handle aboard, as well. Since there was very little way to get the Spanish ship anywhere it could be sold, Markus had the crew transferred to the Irish Rose and locked away.

Charges were set, using some of the Spanish ship's own gunpowder, and as the Irish Rose sailed for the African shore again, the charges blew, and the Spanish ship slipped below the surface.

Although they had favorable winds most of the way back to the coast, they began to change before they reached it. Reach it they did, around midnight, with one of the long boats in the lead, guiding them into a large harbor.

The Spanish crew was transferred ashore, with plenty of provisions, and even two weapons, with the assurance that their whereabouts would be reported. And the Spanish captain was left in possession with a letter for the Spanish authorities.

"Markus?" Aislinn asked her brother once the crew transfer was finished.

She did not have to continue.

"The British crew?" he asked in return. "No. I will not leave them to their fate. Meyer assures me that the storm will be upon us by tomorrow evening. With the ship aground as it is, they have very little hope. I saw at least one of their long boats destroyed when the masts came down. We are headed back there now."

"Thank you," Aislinn said quietly.

Tired as they were, and with only token grumbling, when Markus gave the order to hoist the anchor and set sails the crew did so. Once they were out of the harbor, with clear sailing ahead, Markus turned the wheel over to Hernando, with the authority of Fourth Mate, and ordered half of the crew below to get some sleep, with Ricardo and Meyer following suit. After one last turn around deck, to encourage the men, Markus turned in as well.

The winds had shifted significantly during the early morning hours. When Markus went up on deck the next morning, the winds were more or less parallel to the coast, and the seas were shifting noticeably from the long swells of earlier, to much rougher water.

Markus had no doubts that Meyer was correct when he said the storm approaching was going to be a hurricane, if it was not already. Hernando had positioned the Irish Rose well away from the British frigate, up wind of her, and kept just enough sail up to maintain a figure eight holding course just out of sight of the warship.

Giving it just a bit more time, Markus killed some time thinking, before he gave the orders to add sail, and turned the Irish Rose toward the British frigate. Everyone had been able to get enough rest and eat, so the crew was ready and able to take their fighting stations when the frigate came into sight.

Gun ports were opened and the guns run out, ready if needed. The pumps were manned to keep the bilges cleared of the water that washed in through the ports from time to time as the Irish Rose rolled in the roughening seas.

The British captain was well aware of the peril his men were in. Besides the long boat that Markus had seen destroyed, both of the others, though not destroyed, were damaged badly enough that they would not survive enough trips to get the crew to the shore, along with what they would need to survive until found.

When the Irish Rose appeared again, this time behind and upwind of the frigate, guns at the ready, and her colors up, the British Captain ordered the Union Jack to be lowered. It was despite several objections from a couple of his junior officers.

The Captain held sway. His career was over anyway, with running the frigate aground. Surrendering a ship damaged more than enough to ensure it would be totally destroyed by the time the approaching storm was over, would not make it that much worse. At least not if he could somehow convince the Pirate Captain to have mercy on the frigate's crew.

With strict orders to the junior officers that had protested to stay calm and control themselves, and his second in command keeping an eye on them, the Captain stood ready, his crew armed and ready to fight if the Pirates had plans to slaughter them, when Markus stepped on deck from the Irish Rose.

The Captain breathed a bit easier when Markus took a quick look around, and then met his eyes. He saw what he was sure was compassion in the pirate, which surprised him. As did the quiet, and very respectful, request for the Captain to surrender his sword after assuring him that his crew would be treated well and taken to shore with provisions to sustain them until rescue that would be directed to them arrived.

Believing him, the Captain drew his sword slowly, reversed it, and allowed Markus to take it from his hand. Markus handed it to one of the pirates behind him that the Captain suddenly realized was a woman.

That realization convinced him that this was, in fact, the pirate ship he had been sent to find and destroy, bringing back the crew to face charges that would result in them being hanged.

However, as his crew was transferred first to the Irish Rose, and then ashore, all being watched carefully and under armed guard, but with no abuse of any kind, the Captain became convinced of something else. That the rumors of the Irish Rose's Captain and crew were true.

That though they were a tight and effective crew, in a powerfully armed and very fast ship, they seemed to only take from the Spanish, and then with the minimum amount of force required to accomplish the task. There were rumors also that every time a prize was taken, a letter was left informing the Spanish royalty why they were being attacked. Apparently, it was personal in some way.

Even more amazing to not only the Captain, but the crew, was the fact that when they were put ashore, plenty of provisions were as well, along with weapons to protect themselves with and to hunt to supplement their provisions. Even the Captain's sword was returned to him.

Most surprising was the last person left on the shore. It was not one of the frigate's crew. It was a woman. An English woman. One being treated with great respect by not only the two female pirates, and the rest of the pirate crew, but especially by the Pirate Captain.

The British Captain turned surprised eyes to the Pirate Captain when he approached him one last time. "I surrender to you a citizen of your country, who found herself in dire straits through no fault of her own, and fell into our… care… by chance.

"As our grievance is with the Spanish authorities, she is an innocent to us, and would have been delivered to a safe haven in any course, so if you would be so kind as to accept responsibility of her fate, I am sure she would appreciate the gesture, and being free of our ship."

The Captain studied Markus even more than he already had. Escorted by the two female pirates toward himself and the Pirate Captain, the woman walked proudly up to him and stopped.

"May I introduce Lady Elisabeth Montoya, formerly the Lady Elisabeth Churchill of London. If you accept her into your care, we will take our leave, knowing she is under the full protection of the British Navy."

Markus simply looked at the British Captain. Until he bowed slightly toward Elisabeth, and then looked back at Markus. "She will have the full protection of the British Navy, as well as my person protection."

"Thank you, Captain," Markus replied. He just managed to not turn to Elisabeth, just to see her face for one last time. He marched away, his back stiff, with Aislinn and Morgana preceding him, two of his crew keeping an eye on the rest of the British crew.

Nothing else happened, and two of the Irish Rose's long boats returned safely to the ship, and everyone quickly readied the ship for a fast run to try and avoid the worst of the hurricane that was bearing down on them.

It was a rough few days for the Irish Rose, but she, and the crew, came through with flying colors, with the only damage to the ship being the loss of one storm sail when one of its lines simply parted, due to some defect probably, allowing the flapping sail to tear away from the rest of the lines holding it in place.

Markus had been quieter than usual, even considering the storm. Aislinn had tried to get him to talk, but he gently deflected her each time she tried. She gave up, finally, as Markus seemed to snap out of his mood on his own. Though he still could not seem to bear any mention of Elisabeth and what her fate might have been after leaving her on shore with the British frigate's captain and crew.

Once outside the weather pattern of the hurricane, Markus turned the ship back toward the Caribbean islands. Upon their arrival in Nassau, they made quick work of converting what they did not want of the prize cargo into what they did want.

Then Markus set the Irish Rose on a course to a destination he would not divulge to anyone, not even Aislinn, until they were all the way to the Keys islands off the tip of Florida.

He had timed things so they approached one of the small, uninhabited islands near the southern end of the string just before dark. In the tiny inlet of the island, shielded almost entirely by palm trees growing right up to the edge of the shore in many places, Markus, and on his instructions, Aislinn, Morgana, and Ricardo, left the Irish Rose in a long boat to row to the shore of the inlet early the next morning.

Markus finally explained to the others what he was doing. "We are here to store some of the wealth we have accumulated. We need to find a suitable place for seven of the large trunks, three places for two together, plus one alone. And eight of the smaller trunks, two each individually."

"Two each individually?" Aislinn asked. "I do not quite understand, Markus."

A slight smile on his face, Markus gave a bit more of an explanation. "We are storing the first seven trunks in order to be sure we have the wealth to recover and rebuild our home, when we have arranged for the removal of Chavez and Padilla from its environs.

"The other eight trunks, two for each of us, is to provide for any case where, for whatever reason or reasons, we do not all survive this adventure."

The other three all protested. Especially Ricardo and Morgana. Morgana was nearly begging, tears, though unshed, in her eyes, to not even consider them not being together. Or taking something that all had endeavored together to procure.

Markus was adamant. He simply turned and begin walking again. Finally accepting that he would not change his mind, the three helped search out the four spots for the seven large trunks.

After another pleading discussion, which Markus again simply walked away from after several minutes, to look for a place for his two trunks. With sighs and looks between themselves, Aislinn, Morgana, and Ricardo did the same.

When they met at the longboat shortly after noon, Markus and Ricardo rowed them back to the Irish Rose, all staying silent. Markus called a ship's crew meeting that evening for after their evening meal. During it, Markus explained that 'a few of the shares' of the treasure up to this point for himself, Aislinn, Morgana, and Ricardo were going to be deposited on the island.

Any of the crew that wished to do the same could do so the next day, after the four had done so. Aislinn showed the crew the accounting to date. Of the value of the treasure almost five-eighths was currently aboard the Irish Rose in coin form, and another tenth in small, precious items. Another eighth and a half were in Nassau, being held by people that they trusted. The rest had been distributed to the crew as it was accumulated after conversion each time they stayed at Nassau.

Only six of the crew, plus Hernando and Meyers, chose to take advantage of the opportunity. There was no animosity or accusations of unfairness when the treasure was divided and each crew member took their share. Those that would keep theirs squirreled it away with their gear aboard ship, and the others selected suitable containers in which to bury or otherwise sequester the part of their share of the treasure they planned to leave on the island.

It took all of the next day, and part of another, for everyone to be ready to leave the island. It was a rather boisterously happy crew that sailed the Irish Rose away from that unnamed island.

For another year the Irish Rose, under Markus' command, attacked Spanish treasure shipping. Only twice in that time were they unsuccessful in their endeavors. Both times it was due to unreliable information.

Once they were almost caught when the Spanish Galleon they were after turned out to be escorted by not just one but three Spanish Frigates.

The second time, another pirate had simply beaten them to the prize, since Markus had been told the Galleon would not leave the harbor where it was loaded until four days later than it did.

As their reputation grew, along with more than a few fantastical rumors about both the Irish Rose and three of her crew, they seldom had to do more than raise their colors for a prize to drop theirs, often even when with another ship, even sometimes a small warship.

Markus as Irish Red, Gentleman Pirate of the Caribbean; Aislinn as the beautiful, tiny, redheaded wraith that always seemed to be near him; and Morgana, the giantess that was even more fierce and skilled in battle than any other pirate sailing the seas. Even the Irish Rose was considered to have almost magical powers.

With more treasure accumulated than they had ever dreamed possible, and many of the crew ready to find other lives to live now that they had the wherewithal, Markus and Aislinn discussed their future. Both were feeling somewhat the same as some of the crew.

It was only the fact that Padilla and Chavez were still in control at the Georgia estate that Markus and Aislinn decided to continue their pirate careers, for at least a bit longer.

Aislinn, her fae instincts suddenly on alert, cautioned Markus. "Are you sure?" he asked her.

"Ye know I canna be sure, Markus," Aislinn replied, her Irish brogue heavy with her worry. "I just know that it feels that if we continue into next month, it will be bad for us. Very bad."

Hearing both the worry and concern in his sister's voice, Markus decided then and there, that despite his failure to get the Spanish authorities to do anything about their rogue soldiers, the Lynch family's days of piracy would come to an end very shortly, on their terms.

With that in mind, Markus told those that supplied him with information, and those that converted the various treasures captured into useable form that they would no longer be seeing him.

And the three main sources that had fed him information simply turned to others that were eager for the information. It was the buyers of the treasures that were upset about losing the income from dealing with him. Especially one. Markus had just collected the proceeds from the sale of the Irish Rose's last trip.

"Markus!" admonished Dennis MacKay, "You cannot leave me like this! I need you, son. And you need me. The biggest treasure either of us has ever seen or ever will see, is being put together right now, man! You cannot pass this up! Or deny me the opportunity!"

"I do not want to take the chance, Dennis. Aislinn believes…"

"Your sister… Markus, your sister is… Well… You cannot possibly believe her fairytale predictions of the future."

MacKay knew he had overstepped the line with Markus when Markus' face grew hard, and his eyes flashed anger. "Be very careful, MacKay," Markus warned. "I may not be around here much longer, but I have very good sources. I will not tolerate anyone saying anything like that about my sister."

"Yes, yes, of course!" MacKay, quickly replied. "I meant no disrespect, Markus. But let me tell you about…"

"No," Markus replied, standing. "We are done." With that, Markus picked up the two purses, heavy with gold coins, and walked out of the room.

MacKay was not ready to give up. Believing everyone was just as greedy as he, MacKay quickly called for his man, and had him write out a lengthy description of the opportunity he had tried to explain to Markus.

When it was done, he sent his man to the docks, with a bit of coin and the admonition to be sure the papers made it onto the Irish Rose.

Meyers, not one of those ready to give up the quest for riches quite yet, eagerly took the missive from MacKay's man when it was presented to him. He put it away inside his shirt, to wait for the proper time to bring it up with Markus.

With no destination in mind, just a drive to get away from Nassau and the pirate environment, Markus had the Irish Rose sailing on the next available tide, late in the night.

He set a course northwest to clear the islands, not really realizing his intention of eventually going to Boston.

Markus, in talking to Aislinn, Morgana, Ricardo, and Meyer the next morning, after turning over the wheel to Hernando, did come to the conclusion that Boston would be their destination. They would sell the Irish Rose, divide the spoils for the last time, and everyone go their own way.

Except Meyer was not ready for that. He brought up MacKay's proposal, though without mentioning MacKay. He simply said that someone had approached him with the information, for which he had paid the man a few coins, just because he felt sorry for him.

Markus, tired from the long night and the stress of trying to decide what to do, was not really in the mood to argue and basically cut Meyer off and left. However, Meyer was persuasive. Ricardo and Morgana were not very adamant either way.

Aislinn, still unsure about her feelings about the future, was finally convinced that the opportunity was too good to pass up, since it would be completed before the month was up.

It was she that convinced Markus over the next two days to go along with the plan that Meyer and Ricardo had worked out, with her and Morgana's help. Markus gave in, primarily to please Aislinn. The fact that it was only slightly out of their way, as they headed for Boston up the East Coast of the continent helped.

The information was that two Spanish Treasure Galleons were loaded up with various treasure goods from tribes in Mexico and from tribes much further south, at two ports on the eastern coast of Mexico. They were to meet up on the southeast tip of Florida, take on provisions and water, and travel together to Spain for protection.

The information turned out to be fairly accurate. It was, however, not complete. Several changes had been implemented, in large part due to the Irish Rose's reputation. Even with two Galleons travelling together, the Captains and the ship owners were no longer sure they would be able to bluff the Irish Rose's Captain, nor fight the ship off if it caught them at sea.

Rather than two Galleons, there were four at anchor in the small cove where they had gathered to send in crews to hunt and gather foods and fresh water. They had not expected to encounter the Irish Rose until well into their voyage, as those spying on pirate activity had reported when the Irish Rose had arrived at Nassau just days before, and was not expected to leave for several days.

Markus' decision to abruptly leave only two days after arrival left no time for the information to get to the ships before the Irish Rose did.

When the Irish Rose dropped anchor just north of the cove so a longboat could be lowered and the cove investigated. It was with great surprise that Markus took in the four Galleons, anchored side-by-side, secured together to facilitate the loading and distribution of the food and water that was being collected.

After observing for a while, Markus realized that most of the crews were on shore, leaving only a handful of sailors on board the ships. Deciding to take advantage of the situation when he discovered that, Markus immediately headed the longboat back to the Irish Rose.

It took very little time for the crew to have the Irish Rose under sail when they returned. Sailing boldly into the cove, Markus, as he often did, turned the Irish Rose's broadside to the Spanish ships, in a position where they could not respond in any type of effective way.

There was frantic movement on the Spanish ships when the Irish Rose appeared. A longboat was heading for shore when Markus called over to the ships, ordering them to surrender. Their colors were not up, so Markus ordered them to first raise them, and then to lower them to signify their surrender.

With only one of the four Captains aboard, he was reluctant to do so. Markus did not hesitate when the Captain did. A signal from Markus and Morgana fired one of the twelve-pounders so the cannonball just cleared the closest Spanish ship.

With that, the Spanish Captain quickly had the ship's colors run up and then back down.

With the crew ready, Markus had just enough sail put on, and half the oars shipped to maneuver the Irish Rose against the grouped ships. With so many muskets at the ready, along with the guns on the Irish Rose's rails, the Spanish crews put up no resistance.

With Markus in the lead, Aislinn and Morgana right behind him to supervise the selection and moving of the treasures from the four ships to the Irish Rose they boarded the first ship. Aislinn was selective, since there was no way to take all of the treasure from the four ships.

Markus debated on whether or not to transfer the rest of the treasure to one of the Spanish Galleons and put a crew on it to take it with them. When he felt the first stirrings of the air, and realized a storm was brewing, he made the decision to simply take what they had and go.

He was glad he did so, when Aislinn ran up to him and urgently said, "We must go, Markus! Now. I sense… Something…"

Markus ordered the charges lit, and the Irish Rose crew quickly took their stations, the sails were hoisted, and the Irish Rose sailed away, the charges in the bilges of the four Spanish ships barely audible when they blew and the ships went down.

Once clear of the cove, they were better able to get a feel for the storm approaching. It cut off any attempt to sail toward Nassau, so Markus turned the Irish Rose north, staying off the coast enough to have good winds, but close enough to be able to find a safe harbor if the storm came up onto them. It was still rather slow going.

Slow enough that despite the best efforts of Markus and the crew, and the sailing capability of the Irish Rose, the storm caught them. Markus turned the Irish Rose to run before the winds, headed directly for the best shelter that existed within range.

With the charts that he had, Markus had picked a good cove. It would protect the Irish Rose well. The only problem was that the chart maker, working with the information provided to him, was not aware that there was a shoal just south of the entrance to the cove.

It was far too late for Markus and the crew to correct the course to avoid the shoal when it became visible as they approached, but with the order to drop all sail and masterful steering of the Irish Rose they were able to avoid hitting the shoal for as long as possible.

The Irish Rose did hit the shoal hard enough to run hard aground, but the Irish Rose was well built. There was no significant damage, only some sprung and cracked hull planks that the carpenter assured Markus would be no problem to repair to make the Irish Rose seaworthy, but she was not going to get off that shoal with the winds the way they were.

Markus ordered three of the five long boats loaded with food and water, arms, and gear to enable the crew to survive the weather on shore for some time, and for longer if they could not recover the Irish Rose.

For six days the storm raged, having developed into a hurricane by the third day. When it was obvious that it would, Markus ordered the longboats secured, and packs made up with some of their canvas and lines, so the they could head further inland to look for better protection.

The second day after they had set up a secure camp, Markus noticed that Meyer and two of the crew that he had brought with him when he joined the Irish Rose were gone.

At first, he thought that something might have happened to them, but a thorough search in the area and then the camp found no trace of them, and tellingly, of three of the packs and a portion of the supplies.

"They went after the treasure," Ricardo told Markus after the search. "I know he was less than happy with us abandoning the cove and the ship to come inland."

Markus sighed and nodded. "I think you are right." With the hurricane in full force, hunkered down in the shelters, Markus added, "They are welcome to whatever they can recover. If they can recover anything."

Markus, nor any of the others, had any idea just how accurate his last statement would turn out to be, though they would never know.

Meyer was determined to get as much of the treasure as possible. He had seen how much the wind and waves, along with the higher than normal tides, had already shifted the Irish Rose on the shoal.

Despite the reluctance of the two with him, Meyer had them help rig one of the longboats, and during what turned out to be the time the eye of the hurricane was over the cove, they went out to the Irish Rose. Though the hurricane was not of great intensity, the eye was small, and when the winds of the other side of the eye, blowing in the opposite direction as from before, hit the Irish Rose with the three men on her, it was more than enough to slide the ship off the shoal, into the deep-water seaward. The action of the winds and the sea had moved the Irish Rose enough on the shoal that despite her stout construction, the minor damage of the tough hull worsened and then a plank pulled completely free. That small opening could have been repaired, if anyone had been there to do a temporary patch until conditions moderated, but Meyer was after the treasure, not saving the Irish Rose.

The bilges were already awash, and when the ship slipped from the shoal, more water began to pour in. It poured through the damaged hull then, as water continued to come in, through the gaps in the gun deck gun ports.

Burdened with the heavy chests of gold they had managed to get from the hold where it had been locked away, Meyer and the other two were delayed far too long to escape with both the gold and their lives.

The two sailors released their hold on the chest first, and Meyer realized he would never get it above decks. Like the others, he scrambled for the longboat, but it was too late for the three men to save themselves.

They tumbled into the water, near the longboat, but the wind and waves pounded them against the hull of the Irish Rose. All three drowned, their bodies finally floating clear of the well awash Irish Rose. By the time the Irish Rose sank in the much deeper water off the shoal, pulling down the longboat with it, the three bodies were being carried away out further into the sea, on the tide that was running out, against the winds, which were not strong enough to counter the tide's action on the barely afloat remains.

Once the hurricane had passed over the camp, and the Irish Rose's crew had recovered enough, they headed back to the cove. The sea showed only slowly calming water over the shoal. The Irish Rose was long gone.

Markus, Aislinn, Morgana, Ricardo, his brother and the others that had come from Georgia cared not about the loss. And only a few of the other pirates lamented very much. They all had significant amounts of gold and silver put away, some just up the coast from where they had put in. More than enough for them to gain passage on a ship that would enable them to get to a harbor where they could hire a suitable ship to take them to the other spots where they had buried their private holdings of the treasures that had been distributed.

There was a parting of the ways when the group arrived at the location of the buried treasures and each person had recovered their individual amounts. With only two exceptions, those that had come from Georgia stayed with Markus, Aislinn, and Morgana. Those two went with the other pirates, intent on gaining more of their own treasure trove.

Markus agreed to let them have one of the longboats, and he and the others took the other two, and sailed northward along the Florida coast, stopping often to hunt, fish, gather fruits and other wild edibles, and replenish their water supplies.

At the first port they came to, Ricardo took Hernando and two of the men into the small port city. Having made themselves look like a cross between beggars and down-on-their-luck sailors, the four were able to buy enough clothing, as well as some additional gear without causing a stir, to furnish the others in a manner where they would be able to begin travelling openly. At least, more openly.

Still careful to not reveal any signs of being pirates, even former pirates, the group managed to travel further north without discovery. They found a ship ready to make passage to Boston with some cargo. Ricardo was able to make arrangements for Markus, Aislinn, and Morgana to get aboard as paying passengers, with himself and the others joining the crew to work their passage.

They had decided that would be much better than risking exposing just how much gold and silver they had. The possibility of the crew, of mostly Hispanic and Indian heritage, being able to buy passage would be so remarkable it would draw significant attention to them.

Markus had tried to insist on working for his passage, as well, but Ricardo managed to talk him out of it, saying that it would be just as counter-productive, and much more likely to cause someone to wonder about the red-headed, white Irish crewman that could pass for the infamous pirate captain, Irish Red.

The further away from the southeast coast they went, the less the risks were. Having gone ashore several times at some of the stops that the ship made to off-load and take on different cargos, Markus, Aislinn, and Morgana were able to improve their clothing choices, add much better accoutrements to their gear, and obtain items that the others would need upon their arrival in Boston.

When they did arrive there, they had no problem obtaining lodging for themselves and for all of the crew, though they were all in various much less notable accommodations. With a portion of each of their treasures that was mostly gold, enough silver coinage was obtained locally so they could blend into the area even more easily.

Paying with the silver coins was not at all suspicious. Had everything been gold coin, especially when any but Aislinn, Markus, and Morgana used it, would have caused far too much of a stir.

Still, they kept a rather low profile, with Ricardo maintaining contact with Markus, so they could develop a plan, and then execute it.

It was while Markus was checking on possible passage to England or Ireland, that he ran across a notice that intrigued him. It seemed to be meant for him and Aislinn, although he could not fathom why, or whom might have had it posted at the Harbormaster's offices.

There were no names, of course, but the wording, as well as some of the things otherwise mentioned, were easily recognizable to Markus as pertaining to the Irish Rose, and by connection, himself and Aislinn.

He took down the notice when no one was nearby, and took it back to their lodgings with him. Once he arrived, he sat down with Aislinn and they began to puzzle out whatever it was they were reading.

Suddenly Aislinn exclaimed, "It is from Lady Elisabeth, Markus! I am sure of it!"

"From Elisabeth?" Markus murmured. Aislinn took delightful note of his use of Elisabeth's given name.

"I am sure, Markus." She turned in her chair and called Morgana over.

"Morgana. Read this. Do you not think it is from Lady Elisabeth?"

Morgana studied the notice for long moments, reading it silently and then aloud several times, running the words through her mind.

She nodded firmly. "Yes. It is so. See the references? Only she would know these things. It is her." Morgana looked at the excited Aislinn, and the stunned Markus. Hiding a smile, unlike Aislinn's, Morgana went back to what she was doing.

"But how?" asked Markus. "And why?"

"We will know as soon as we dispatch a reply and get her response. Morgana," Aislinn said over her shoulder, "my correspondence box."

Morgana brought over the newly acquired wooden case that held pens, ink, parchment, protective paper, and postage.

"How will we know where to send it?" Markus asked. "There is no real address there."

Aislinn smiled. "Oh, the address is there. I have already figured out that, too."

"But…"

Quickly seeing that Markus would not only not be any help with the missive, but a rather major hindrance, considering what Aislinn wanted to say, she told him, "Markus! Go away. Let me do this."

"But if you give away…"

"I am not going to give away anything that could get us into trouble. I know how to say what I… we… need to say so we can make further contact with her. Trust me. Please."

Markus decided that would be best. Primarily because he was already tongue tied just thinking about Elisabeth. He had no clue what to say to her. When Aislinn handed him the letter, carefully wrapped to hide the address and ready to be posted, he did not protest, nor ask her to open it back up so he could read it. It did not occur to him to open the outer protective wrapping, either. He simply took it to where a street urchin often lingered that could be trusted to get correspondence to a rider that carried mail for hire. With coin in hand for the man, and another for himself, the boy took off running.

Then next time Ricardo met them for dinner, wearing his finest, Markus started to explain about the notice. But Aislinn quickly took over. Dinner was over by the time Markus was able to get a word in edgewise. And it was by then far too late. Aislinn had already convinced Ricardo of the plan they would be following for the next several days, until Lady Elisabeth contacted them again.

When Ricardo rose and left, and Markus was escorting Aislinn and Morgana back to their lodgings, Markus suddenly stopped. "Wait," he said. "You implied that we would know something in a few days. It could take weeks, even months, for the letter to get to Lady Elisabeth in Spain. Or England. You never said where she was living."

"She is living in Boston, Markus," Aislinn said, unable to hold back the lengthy laughing spell at the expression on Markus' face when she told him that.

Only a quelling look from Markus stopped Morgana's laughter, and it did nothing to stop her grin.

"Let's go," Markus finally said, taking both women's arms in his, to hurry them back to their lodgings.

Once there, and cloaks hung and a fire started, Markus finally cornered Aislinn, who had made it a bit of a game of avoiding Markus since their arrival. "Yes, Markus? You wanted to speak to me?"

Markus nearly growled, causing Aislinn to smile. "Fine, Markus. I am sorry. What is it you want to know?"

"Elis… Lady Elisabeth is in Boston? Are you sure? How do you know?" Markus sounded between forlorn and agonizingly anxious.

Aislinn sat down in a chair before the fire, and Markus sat next to her in another of the chairs. "I am sure of it, Markus," Aislinn replied calmly. "She is staying with one of the families on the hill here in Boston. The Fitzsimons."

"How did you figure that out?" Markus asked.

Aislinn grinned. "It's a woman thing, Markus. There were some clues that only another woman would understand. But believe me. That notice was from Elisabeth, and she is here in Boston. And will reply within a few days. I am sure of it."

Markus leaned back in the chair slightly and seemed to relax. Aislinn decided to stir the pot just a bit. "It will be really nice to see her under better circumstances. And I am anxious to see who might be courting her now that her period of mourning is over."

"What?" exclaimed Markus. He was suddenly sitting up straighter, on the edge of the chair. "Being courted? You think she is? That someone…" Markus fell silent, his gaze lost in the distance.

Aislinn smiled, but quickly hid it when Markus looked at her again, a stricken look on his face.

"Of course, I have no idea. It is just that she is a beautiful woman. She should have a husband. And I am sure it will not take her long to find one." Aislinn cut her eyes to Markus and then back away. He was watching her, his eyes large.

"I would imagine she must have a dozen suitors. Probably more. Elisabeth would just have to make a decision, I suspect."

"Oh…" Markus said.

Aislinn could hear the near despair in his voice. "Good," Aislinn thought to herself. "He is now going to be thinking about the situation, very seriously."

With that, Markus excused himself and went to his room to think. And think he did. It was well after midnight when he finally came to a decision. After that, he was able to fall asleep without further problems.

CHAPTER SIX

Markus did not have to wait long to begin implementing his plan. He did have a few qualms, but he suppressed them quickly upon his first view of Lady Elisabeth Montoya.

She had just entered the parlor of the house Markus was renting, after Morgana answered the door upon hearing the knock. Markus' eyes passed over the man and woman accompanying her, and settled on Elisabeth. It was as if he was drinking in the finest Irish spring water when he looked at her.

Elisabeth had a hug for Morgana, and then tears and a long, hard hug when Aislinn came into the parlor, having heard the knock as well. Without realizing it, Markus took the final three steps down the stairs, his eyes still on Elisabeth.

Apparently, the movement was enough to draw Elisabeth's attention. When she glanced in his direction, she, like Markus, only had eyes for him, just the way he did for her.

Markus stopped again, as Elisabeth turned and took a step toward him, but she stopped as well. Neither said a word, but their eyes were locked on one another. For what seemed an agonizingly long time there was total silence.

Suppressing the smile that was trying to form, Aislinn broke the silence. She stepped forward, and said, "Markus, you remember Lady Montoya?"

Markus started. "Of course!" he managed to say without shouting, giving Aislinn a look that asked her if she was crazy. He moved forward, stopping before Elisabeth. He made a slight bow. "Lady Montoya. It is nice to see you again. You look well."

"Thank you, Captain Lynch. And I have taken my maiden name again. Churchill. But please. You may call me Elisabeth."

When she held out her hand, Markus took it. "Miss… Elisabeth. Yes. Of course. And, please. Call me Markus. I no longer have a ship. I cannot claim the title of Captain."

Markus realized that he still held Elisabeth's hand. He loosened his grip, though it was not at all tight, but Elisabeth made no move to remove her hand. It was Markus that, reluctantly, slid his hand away from hers.

"As you wish, Markus. It is good to see you. I am sorry about the Irish Rose. Aislinn said you lost her in a storm."

"Yes," Markus replied, "But it is of no matter. That life is behind me. All of us, actually, that were involved."

"That is good to know, Markus," replied Elisabeth. She cut her eyes to the other two people that had entered the house with her. "I must remember my manners. May I introduce the Fitzsimmons? Richard and Katherine. Markus Lynch."

Markus and Aislinn went through the process of being introduced and greeting the Fitzsimmons formally. It was Aislinn that suggested that she and Markus would make sure Elisabeth would be seen back to the Fitzsimmons' home later, if the Fitzsimmons wished to leave.

Immediately after the Fitzsimmons left, Aislinn got Elisabeth and Markus sitting very close to each other in the parlor, with Morgana getting refreshments. Aislinn sat beside Elisabeth, but made sure Elisabeth kept her attention on Markus.

After a bit of small talk, Elisabeth said, "I really am very sorry about the Irish Rose. She was a wonderful ship. But I am so very glad that you are no longer in that environment. I know you did not fully achieve your goal."

Aislinn watched Markus closely, as well as Elisabeth. The two were now focused on each other. "No," Markus replied. "But we have come out of it with more than what our place in Georgia is worth."

Markus paused and looked away. "I do hate the fact that I have allowed someone to drive me from my property. And failed to achieve a goal I set for myself.

I do wish to find something to do with myself. I want… need… to be out in the wilds. I feel so… constricted."

He winced suddenly, and looked back at Elisabeth. "I…"

"I understand, Markus." Elisabeth's voice was soft. She was watching his face. "And Markus… I understand the risks to you. Not just when you were… were in the Caribbean, but now, if anyone was to find out…"

Markus was shaking his head. "Do not concern yourself, Elisabeth." With a grimace, Markus added, just now realizing the fact that his original plan was unworkable, "And speaking of that, I believe you should disassociate yourself from us."

He glanced over at Aislinn and saw her consternation. "From me, I mean me. I think associating with Aislinn and Morgana… and the others… you would be safe. But with me… if I am discovered, and there is any type of connection between us, you could be in great danger."

Elisabeth was shaking her head. "No, Markus. That is just it. I have been able to prevent that. It is not a danger now. To me or to you."

"What?" Aislinn asked, despite her intention to keep Markus and Elisabeth talking.

Elisabeth glanced at Aislinn, but her attention went back to Markus. "Markus," she said urgently, both her hands going to take one of Markus' as she leaned forward earnestly. "I have worked with both the Spanish and English governments. You have been pardoned, Markus!"

Another glance at Aislinn. "And you. Everyone on the Irish Rose."

Looking back at Markus, Elisabeth saw his stunned look. "But… You can't… They would never just pardon a pirate, Elisabeth." Markus looked resolute.

"It is true, Markus. I have the documents. It took me a year to accomplish. First the Crown. They were reluctant, at first, of course, but Captain Smythe, Winston… agreed to lend his support to my effort. He was impressed with your… character…

and despite being forced out of the Navy, he was… and is… still held in very high esteem.

"And since the activities were all directed against the Spanish, and you showed great mercy to captives, the Admiralty finally agreed to remove you from the list of those wanted for piracy. You are in no danger from the English government."

Elisabeth regretted the loss of Markus's hand when he leaned back in his chair beside the settee she and Aislinn shared. "Be that as it may," he said after a moment, "I have doubts about the Spanish Crown doing the same."

"Are you calling Elisabeth a liar?" asked Aislinn, just to get a reaction.

Markus leaned forward, his eyes going to Elisabeth's again, after a quick, hard look at his sister. "No! Of course not! Elisabeth would never lie!" His voiced faded to one much less forceful. "It is just… I just do not see how they would be willing to agree…"

He had dropped his eyes, but they went back to Elisabeth's. He could see the sincerity when she spoke, having again taken one of Markus' hands in hers when he leaned forward and she could reach them.

"I am not lying, Markus. And you are correct. I would never lie about this. My former husband, may he rest in peace, was a powerful Hidalgo in Spain before he became a diplomat. And he was well respected in that capacity, as well. And, as his widow, I was shown nearly the same respect.

"After explaining the actions of those two cretins to several of my acquaintances in the diplomatic corps, they supported me in my petition to the Crown to see justice done.

"I will admit that it was difficult. Very difficult." Elisabeth looked away for a moment. When Markus squeezed her hand in sympathy she smiled slightly and looked back at him.

"But I was determined. And persistent. I was finally able to gain an audience with someone in a position to do something about the situation. When I explained what I knew, And Captain Smythe added his testimony, and information I had requested from here in the New World finally arrived, he agreed to take it to his superiors for consideration."

"It was an agonizing month and a half, but I finally received word to return for another meeting." Elisabeth sighed. "Unfortunately, there was no willingness to actually do anything about your property.

"They consider the regular soldiers… just deserters, and if they go back to Florida and are found, they will be arrested as deserters. The two officers, however, they consider traitors that have committed treason.

"They still will not do anything about them, unless they were to return to Florida, or in the unlikely event, Spain. In either case, they would be arrested and hanged.

"But there is very little they are willing to do to even try to help recover your property. They have basically just written the soldiers off and are ignoring the whole situation in Georgia. The only thing that might be an option is if we, not they, can find a Spanish official here in America somewhere willing to go there and give them the official word they are to return to Spain to be arrested, they will allow it."

Markus and the others looked discouraged. "They would never agree to that!" Markus exclaimed. "It would mean their death. And I have doubts there are any Spaniards that would be willing to face them. Chances are the man would simply be shot and buried."

Elisabeth sighed. "I know. It is unlikely to happen." Suddenly Elisabeth's face lighted up with a broad smile. "There is great news, as well. All the papers and documents concerning you, Aislinn, Morgana, and the crew, were ready for me. All signed, and with the seals in place. You are a free man, Markus. As are all of you and the others."

Markus' eyes went wide. "Truly?" he asked.

"Truly," she replied, just as softly.

Aislinn thought that Markus was actually going to kiss Elisabeth, as both had leaned forward, and their faces were only inches apart. Markus, realizing that he was actually about to do that very thing, leaned back and let his hand slide from Elisabeth's.

Elisabeth blushed slightly as she straightened up in the settee. She had to clear her throat twice before she could speak. "Yes. I shall bring the documents to you, at your convenience. But perhaps I should go now."

When Elisabeth started to rise, Markus leapt to his feet, extending a hand to assist her. Aislinn quickly protested. "Oh, you must stay, Elisabeth. Morgana and I have had great success with some new cooking skills. Dinner will not be long from now."

Aislinn glanced between the two of them. "Perhaps you and Markus could go over a few… things… in the meantime."

"I don't think Elis…"

When Markus started to speak for her, Elisabeth's chin when up slightly. "Why, that does sound delightful," she said, not looking at Markus, but making sure he was well aware that she was no shrinking wallflower. She could, and would, stand up for herself.

"Of course," Markus said, recovering quickly. "But I must decline any further discussion at the moment. I must attend to several things in the stable with Ricardo." He bowed slightly toward Elisabeth, and turned toward the stairs.

Aislinn tried to think of something to keep Markus near, but Elisabeth was already saying, "If you would, Markus, please inform the others of the pardons. That they need not fear for their safety in terms of their activities in the Caribbean."

Markus turned back toward Elisabeth, one foot on the lowest step. "Of course, Elisabeth. I shall." Her broad smile had an even bigger one on his face when he went up the stairs.

"Come," Aislinn said, linking an arm with Elisabeth's. "I know it is not proper form to entertain in the kitchen, but I believe that you would not mind a bit. It will let us catch up with each other. And I am sure Morgana is aching to hear everything, as well."

Markus did spend a bit of time in the stables, going over several things with Ricardo, about some horses they were contemplating acquiring. Making sure he had plenty of time to accomplish an errand and get back in time for the evening meal, Markus saddled his stallion and rode toward the Boston shopping district.

He was home, and changed for dinner in plenty of time. It was difficult to control his emotions during the meal, to which Ricardo had been invited. To Markus' amazement, Elisabeth seemed to fit right in with the rather homey scene, talking animatedly with Ricardo, as well as Aislinn and Morgana.

Markus was quiet most of the meal, his eyes more often on Elisabeth than elsewhere. And every time their eyes met, she had a smile for him, which he returned.

Not long after the meal was over, another knock came on the front door of the house. Despite Aislinn's assurances that Elisabeth would be escorted back to the Fitzsimmons' home, one of their carriages and driver had been sent to pick her up.

Aislinn frowned, but as Markus allowed Elisabeth to take his arm to accompany her out, the frown faded. She quickly said good-bye, as did Morgana. Both were watching through a tiny gap in the curtains when Markus handed Elisabeth into the carriage.

Morgana and Aislinn exchanged a quick glance when they saw Markus put a hand on the window edge of the carriage after Elisabeth had settled herself inside. He had leaned forward, and both women could see that Elisabeth had leaned forward, as well, so she could hear what he was saying.

And both women saw the huge smile on Elisabeth's face when she nodded hugely and said a few words. Then Elisabeth's gloved hand rested on top of

Markus' for a moment, as he gave word to the driver that Elisabeth was ready. He stepped back and watched the carriage drive away until it was out of sight.

When he turned back toward the house, Aislinn was delighted to see the contented smile on Markus' face. One she recognized as always following accomplishing something he had set out to do.

"Well now," Aislinn said when Markus had come back inside, the grin still on his face. "You seem rather happier now than before Elisabeth arrived."

"Of course," Markus replied. "She brought us very good news." Markus was feeling great, and decided to aggravate Aislinn and Morgana. At least a little. He would not go so far as risk bodily harm from Aislinn, which was entirely possible if he withheld his information too long.

"I am quite pleased with that. Aren't you?"

"Well, of course I am!" Aislinn said, hands on her hips, but with a frown curving her lips rather than a smile.

"That is good, then," Markus said. "I think I shall go up to bed. I have many things to accomplish on the morrow."

"But what did…" Morgana burst out, but quickly blushed and fell silent. It was certainly not her place to question her charge's brother.

Aislinn came through for her, though that was not her primary intent. Aislinn wanted to know, for herself. "What did you and Elisabeth discuss at the carriage?"

Markus waved a hand dismissively. "Oh that. I simply asked Elisabeth's permission to pay her court. Elisabeth agreed. Quite graciously, I might add."

Aislinn squealed and leaped into Markus' arms. "Oh, I am so pleased! I have been orches…" Aislinn fell silent when Markus put her back down on the floor and gave her a stern look.

"You, my sister, shall cease and desist from any attempts to influence my future bride. Whatever might come to pass, she and I, will be making our decisions all by ourselves, without any interference from you."

Markus looked over at Morgana, who blushed first, and then went pale. "Or your minions," he added.

Aislinn looked a bit chagrinned, but not enough to satisfy Markus that Aislinn, and possibly Morgana as well, would not try to speed up the process or alter it in some way.

Markus shook his finger at Aislinn. "You just let me handle things. On my own timetable and in my own way."

"Of course, Markus," Aislinn replied, putting the most innocent look on her face she could manage.

Markus groaned slightly, but left it at that. He turned away, without saying anything else and headed up to his bedroom. Aislinn turned to Morgana and the two grinned widely, and began to eagerly discuss the situation. And how they could make things go quickly and smoothly.

Aislinn was including Morgana in more and more things, which Morgana was now accepting without resisting, having said for such a long time that her place was as a servant, and not an equal. With everything that had occurred over the last years, she realized she simply was as much, if not more, Aislinn's friend than handmaiden.

Even Markus was treating her as such, almost as a member of the family. As she thought about it, Ricardo, Hernando and essentially all of the others, were treating her as their equal, and as Aislinn's friend, much as Ricardo was Markus' friend as much as employee.

Over the next several weeks, Markus and Elisabeth spent as much time courting, chaperoned either by Aislinn or the Fitzsimmons, as they did arranging to go to Georgia to take back the Lynch property from Capitán Padilla and Teniente Chavez.

The one thing that was a bone of contention between Markus and Elisabeth, and annoyed Aislinn no end, was Markus' absolute refusal to get married to Elisabeth until after he was again master of the Lynch property, but he was adamant.

When the arrangements were finally made to head for Georgia, Elisabeth traveled with them as his fiancée, with Aislinn and Morgana her chaperones.

The initial journey was by ship, from Boston to the bay which had shipped so much of the property's production under Markus' guidance. From there they traveled by horseback, with wagons carrying the equipment and supplies they were taking with them.

Aislinn was finding herself a bit distracted by the Spaniard that Elisabeth had arranged to go with them through her contacts in the Spanish diplomatic corps. Senõr Antonio Montebon was a handsome young man. And very personable. And spoke excellent English. And was very attentive to her. Despite Markus' warnings to both of them about anything happening that should not.

Elisabeth often had a smile on her face when she looked over at Aislinn and Antonio riding side by side, talking. It was a different smile than the one she had for Markus, as he led the group on his horse.

Morgana, well aware of the attraction between her charge and the Spaniard had decided fairly quickly that he was a worthy suitor, and made sure she kept an eye on them, but gave Aislinn enough space and privacy for her to get to know the man.

Ricardo and Hernando were again in charge of the rest of the group headed back to their home. All were eager to arrive. And all were more than willing to do whatever was necessary to re-take the property from the interlopers that were now in control.

They had received enough information during the time they were gone that they were well aware of the way the locals were being treated. Each man that had left behind any family was eager to extract justice for the wrongs done their families.

Markus stopped the group well away from the property. Although he wanted desperately to go to investigate the situation himself, Ricardo had little trouble convincing him that it would be a much better if he allowed Ricardo to do the reconnaissance.

Ricardo would be able to contact his family and the others that had stayed behind, and find out much of what was needed to allow them to take back the property.

Ricardo looked grim when he returned after a week away from the camp. Markus, Elisabeth, Aislinn, Morgana, Hernando, and Antonio joined him in the main camp's large tent.

Ricardo cut his eyes to the women, but sighed slightly. They would not be excluded. "It is not good, Señor. Padilla and Chavez rule with an iron hand. The soldiers… they are no longer soldiers. They are simply Padilla's and Chavez's henchmen.

"A few left early on. The rest have become little more than animals. Only a few of our people are left in the area. And they are men, there simply to keep an eye on the place, waiting for our return."

Markus looked surprised. "They expected us to return?"

A small smile curved Ricardo's lips. "Of course, Señor. When we left, the ones that did not come with us knew that we would one day return for you to retake your rightful place as owner of the property, and once again bring peace and prosperity to all who live here."

Markus was taken aback by Ricardo's words. And even more so when Hernando added, "And the rest of our families, who have waited patiently in Florida, are already on their way here, to resume their lives."

"But…" Markus said, uncertain. Elisabeth took his hand and gave it a squeeze. Markus looked at her, and then Aislinn and Morgana.

"You have great confidence in my ability to regain the property."

Ricardo smiled. "Oh, Señor, you have not the least idea of how many of us feel about you and the Señorita. There is no doubt about your ability to triumph, now that you need not fear for innocent lives."

Markus met Ricardo's eyes, and felt the trust the man had for him. He could not fail these people. Far more than employees, even before their recent activities. He gave a slight nod, which satisfied Ricardo, and prompted him to continue his report.

"Though there are still a few of our people involved, as I said, all the rest have moved beyond Padilla's reach. His soldiers tried to do the work when they took over and our people were gone. That is when several soldiers left. Of those that stayed, Padilla and Chavez sent a few out to round up everyone they could.

"Our people stayed hidden, and only those that had no idea what they were going to be subjected to agreed to work. And many were simply taken, and made to work. Again, several managed to get away. The rest that work are virtual slaves, kept within the confines of the property.

"Their families, those that have not fled, are in dire straits. Chavez has taken many women. Some did not survive the ordeals. Everyone in the area is terrified of him. Though none of the others are as bad as he, they have been given free rein to do as they want when off the property.

"Because of the treatment by Chavez, and general ineptitude of Padilla, they are unable to produce more than a fraction of what you were able to ship to the coast. They even have trouble feeding themselves well. There is very little stock, and all of it is in poor condition. And only Padilla's and Chavez's personal mounts are well attended. The other horses and oxen are barely able to work, and many have been treated badly. Very badly."

Markus' face had become hard the others noted. It was a moment before he spoke. He turned to look at Antonio Monteban. "You will be at great risk if you present yourself in your official capacity. I will not ask you to do that. There is no chance that any of them will offer themselves up for arrest."

Montebon stood proud and firm. "I will perform my duty, sir. They are my countrymen, and if they have brought dishonor to my country, I shall do what I must to rectify the situation, and bring them to justice. And it is quite obvious that what they have done is far beyond bringing dishonor to Spain. They appear to be animals that must be put down."

Aislinn was beaming, for a moment, until the complete meaning of what Montebon was saying struck her. She paled when it did. Antonio, like Markus, would beard the lion in its den, without question. She started to speak up in protest, but both Elisabeth and Morgana, though they shared much the same understanding, took her hands, and she stayed silent.

"When?" Markus asked, looking over at Ricardo.

This time Ricardo's smile was feral. "Day after tomorrow. At noon. Padilla and Chavez always do an inspection of the shipments before they leave for the coast. The next one is scheduled to leave day after tomorrow. It will be another small one, but they are desperate to get income, and often ship whenever they have even one wagonload."

"I am curious," Antonio said, "Who do they trust enough to make the shipments?"

"No one," Ricardo replied. "They have some they trust a bit more than others. Only because they send enough of the former soldiers, led by Chavez, to make sure they get there with the goods, and back with the money.

"There is speculation that Chavez has been taking a small portion of the sales, without Padilla knowing. It is not certain, but that is the rumor."

Antonio looked disgusted. "I see. It is time that this is ended. Day after tomorrow I will do my duty and present the orders. If they refuse, I will assist in whatever way you might request to achieve the task of removing them from the property and installing you and your people back to rightful ownership."

Markus hesitated only a moment before he nodded. "Very well. You and I shall confront them together day after tomorrow."

As expected by both Markus and Antonio, who had already learned that the women associated with Markus were unlike any he had ever known, and would protest, vocally, the plan just expressed, faced the others and listened patiently to those protests.

The protests were ignored, and Markus, Antonio and Ricardo left the women behind and went to make their plans. It was the only time in a very long time that Markus had refused to include Aislinn, and even Morgana in planning something.

That made little difference. If anything, it encouraged the two to make their own plans. Of course, Elisabeth was included in their plan making now.

Everyone was up early the day the confrontation would take place. Markus was a tad worried when neither Aislinn nor Elisabeth asked anything about the plan the three men had come up with. Both went about the regular morning routine, along with Morgana.

Markus put it out of his mind shortly after breakfast, when he and Antonio went to talk to Ricardo, to set up what he and the rest of the men would be doing during the meeting.

Markus gave strict orders for Ricardo to stay out of the confrontation, other than preventing any interference by any of those with Capitán Padilla and Teniente Chavez. If Antonio's orders were rejected, which was expected, Markus would deal with the two men.

And Markus was well prepared to do so. He had been very good with all of his weapons before everything happened. And he, like the others, had honed those skills over the months and years of piracy.

With three large bore flintlock pistols, freshly loaded and primed, his saber sharpened to almost a razor edge, and the several knives he had on his person were just as sharp, if not sharper.

Since it was a matter of honor, Markus and Antonio both took great care with their appearance as they prepared for the confrontation. Though Markus had never been one to be particularly concerned about his appearance, on this day he decided he would present the strongest image he could achieve. Antonio had decided much the same thing.

None of the women had even an inkling of those thoughts that had run through the men's minds. From their location, out of sight of the tent from which Markus and Antonio stepped, all three gasped slightly.

Where Antonio was regally dressed, in official splendor as a Spanish government official conducting Crown business, Markus on the other hand, was more than a bit flamboyant.

Markus had polished his tall leather boots that went high up his thighs, even with the uppers turned down into a wide cuff. The trousers he wore were one of the many pairs he had commissioned one of the seamstresses in Nassau to make for him from some of the fabulous fabrics they had captured from some of the treasure ships that had come around the Horn. These were a deep, coal black.

His shirt, also silk, was more flowing, and a brilliant green that, Elisabeth noted, matched his eyes perfectly. On his hands Markus wore polished, cuffed leather gauntlets.

A bright red sash was around his waist, over which was his black leather sword belt with polished brass buckle.

On his head was the wide brimmed, beaver felt hat, black, with three colorful tropical bird feathers adorning it.

His leather baldric, with the three pistols, was polished as brightly as his boots and all the other leather gear he wore. It was attached to his sword belt to give additional support to Markus' saber, carried in its polished scabbard.

Elisabeth was not the only one that drew a sharp breath, holding it without realizing it when the men appeared. Elisabeth's eyes were for Markus. Aislinn, in the same state, could not take her eyes off Antonio.

An amused Morgana was impressed with the two, but her eyes were drawn to Ricardo. Holding the horses for Markus and Antonio, receiving a last few instructions, he was dressed as he normally was. Ready for any type of work that Markus might ask him to accomplish.

While not embellished, Morgana had come to expect his trim, neat appearance at all times, with well-fitting clothing, kept in good repair and clean. She did note that he was dressed in his finest set of clothing.

The other two finally released their breaths as Markus and Antonio rode off. Morgana sighed, without realizing it, when Ricardo walked off into the forest.

It was a few moments before the three women were able to speak. Wwhen they did, it was quick and whispered. All three headed toward the horses that they had saddled earlier, leaving them well out of sight of the camp.

All three drew up short when they came into the small clearing where the horses were hobbled, grazing on the lush grass. Ricardo was there, a slight smile on his face as the three women slowed their pace and approached him.

For some reason of which they were not quite sure, Elisabeth and Aislinn cut their eyes to Morgana. Somewhat to their surprise, as well as her own, it was Morgana that spoke to Ricardo.

"You will not stop us, you know," Morgana told Ricardo. "We… They… will not stand idly by and see them harmed, without doing our part to prevent it."

"They are fearful of you being harmed," Ricardo replied, but his eyes, they all noted, were on Morgana's.

"And we, they. So… what is it you are planning, to prevent us from going and assisting them?"

"Not a thing, Señoras," Ricardo replied, sparing barely a glance at the other two, his eyes once again going to Morgana. "Perhaps an assist to mount…?" Ricardo cupped his hands and crouched slightly beside Morgana's large gelding.

Morgana's only comment was a slightly lifted eyebrow. She stepped forward and upward, her boot finding his hand unerringly. As he boosted slightly, Morgana seated herself astride the large animal, all three women having taken to riding in the same manner as the men, unless they were dressed for social occasions, where they still rode side saddle in their dresses.

It did not seem to be a problem for any of the men, as all three women wore suitable garments to allow the astride style of riding without any hint of impropriety. And they were respected for it by the men. All had come to know and understand just how capable and resolved they were, to work just as hard at the jobs as they did themselves.

As Morgana held the gelding steady, Ricardo seated Elisabeth on her mare, and then Aislinn on Spirit. Both knew she could have easily mounted, but it seemed to be something Ricardo wanted to do, so Aislinn allowed it.

Though he stood still to watch the women ride out of the small clearing, he was running when he left, to get to the point where he and the other men would be, ready to take a hand in the situation, if required, no matter what Markus had said. Not only was this land theirs, through association with Markus and Aislinn, but the area was their home, and had been for many years.

Confident of their success, the families were already in the process of leaving Florida and heading back home, lock, stock, and barrel. Ricardo found himself smiling slightly when he met up with Hernando, the men ready to go.

With the three women out of sight on one side of the staging area, and Ricardo and the other men on the other, Antonio and Markus rode slowly into the clearing from the direction the shipment would be going.

The men there with the two wagons watched cautiously. They turned when Padilla and Chavez rode into the clearing, pulling up their galloping horses cruelly to a sliding stop.

There were four former soldiers with the two. They marched into the clearing just after Padilla and Chavez rode in. "You!" Padilla said, almost yelling. His free hand went to his right thigh, where Markus had run him through in their first fight.

Chavez was itching to attack, thinking, correctly, that if Markus was around, Aislinn would not be far away.

Padilla opened his mouth to speak again, but Antonio spoke first.

"Capitán Padilla and Teniente Chavez, as the appointed representative of your King, I am ordering you to surrender yourselves to me, for return to Spain to face charges of desertion and treason…"

Padilla looked slightly taken aback, but Antonio's words seemed to have infuriated Chavez. Before Padilla could do anything, Chavez spurred his horse, drew his sword, and charged Markus.

Markus did not hesitate. It took only a subtle movement of his knees and Leprechaun leaped forward, more than ready to meet the charge. Markus drew his saber, and with a feral smile leaned slightly forward, urging Leprechaun onward.

Where Chavez was screaming and swinging his sword wildly, Markus was silent, and held his saber in a low ready position. As the two approached each other, Markus guided Leprechaun with his knees, guiding the big stud to pass Chavez on his right.

Chavez drew back his sword, intending to make a hard swing forward and down at Markus' lower chest, hoping to slice his stomach wide open, but Markus and Leprechaun were a practiced pair. As Leprechaun sped past the other horse, Markus leaned far forward and down, to the right, lifting the tip of his saber slightly.

Chavez' wild swing swept well over Markus' back as the tip of Markus' saber slid into his side, and as both horses galloped forward, Markus' sword pivoted slightly, cutting a long gash in Chavez' side. Chavez screamed, dropped his sword, and grabbed his side as he fell from his now panicked horse.

Padilla had recovered quickly. He already had one of his pistols out and was aiming it at Markus, but Markus expected the move, and with a knee movement had turned Leprechaun toward the Spanish Captain.

Managing to get the shot off, Padilla's horse had shied as the large stallion approached, making the shot go wide. Padilla threw down the first pistol and was drawing another, but Markus' saber, missing Padilla as he swept past, did nick Padilla's horse.

Padilla's horse reared in pain, and Padilla rolled off the back, losing the second pistol. When Markus pulled Leprechaun to a stop and spun the horse around, he saw Padilla on the ground, reaching for the pistol.

Markus swung his left leg up and over the saddle, and slid to the ground, saber still in hand. He was too far away to keep Padilla from getting to the dropped pistol. A shot rang out, and the pistol spun further away. Both men's eyes went to the side of the clearing. Aislinn stood there with a musket in her hand, smoke still curling from the muzzle.

She was handing it to Morgana to reload, and accepting another loaded one from Elisabeth.

"Seems to be steel to steel," Markus said to Padilla, slowly approaching him as Padilla stood up, drawing his sword. "Again," Markus added. He made a small movement with his saber and Padilla flinched, his sword swinging back and forth before him.

"Makes no difference, bastardo," Padilla said. "Even if I do not run you through, my men will take you down, and your sister… and the other women… You will pay for your insolence and interference."

"I am not worried," Markus said calmly. "I have a few men, as well, and while they will not intervene in our activities, they will see to it that the land is once again worked by men that have the best interest of the local people at heart."

Ricardo stepped into the clearing then, some distance from Aislinn, Morgana, and Elisabeth. He made a slight, but obvious, motion with one hand and several of the men showed themselves around the edge of the clearing, making sure Padilla and his men all saw them, before stepping back out of sight.

Padilla was looking decidedly worried now, but he advanced on Markus, his sword up, talking the entire time. Making threats, blustering, trying to distract Markus. He almost did when he mentioned Aislinn.

Apparently, he had taken note of Elisabeth, as well, and when he mentioned 'the third woman', Markus' obvious reaction gave Padilla hope. He continued to talk about her, but Markus was able to ignore it.

When Padilla lunged, Markus parried and managed to nick Padilla in his left arm with his counter move. Padilla backed off; a bit warier now. Markus pressed the attack.

Markus had to admit that Padilla was an excellent swordsman. And now that Padilla realized he was fighting for his life, he reverted to his training and concentrated on his fighting skills, going silent except for the occasional grunt or other sound as he fought Markus.

As good as Padilla was, and now fighting for his life, Markus was better, and had even more incentive than Padilla. Padilla was worried only about his own life. Markus felt the responsibility for the lives of his sister, Morgana, Elisabeth, and all of his employees and their families. His own life was not nearly as much of a consideration to him, as long as he protected the others.

It was not long before Padilla had several minor wounds, blood showing all over his clothing. Desperate now, Padilla's training slipped and he began to get wild. His savage swings and lunges simply left him open to Markus' precision attacks.

With everyone concentrating on Markus and Padilla, no one noticed Chavez, still down, slowly draw a pistol from inside his shirt. It was covered with blood from his wound, but his hand was steady enough to aim it at Markus, who was still for a moment, waiting for Padilla to make another move.

Antonio saw Chavez at the very last moment and yelled to warn Markus, even as he rushed toward Chavez. Chavez fired, and Antonio went down, the ball meant for Markus going into Antonio's hip.

Aislinn screamed and ran toward the fallen Antonio. Morgana calmly lifted the reloaded musket and put a finishing ball in Chavez' head. At Aislinn's scream and the sound of the shot, Markus started to turn his head, but saw Padilla making a move.

Markus turned back to meet the charge head on, and deflected Padilla's sword, just barely. The impact staggered Markus and he went to one knee. That was Padilla's chance. He dropped his sword and drew his third, hidden pistol and aimed at Markus once more.

Ricardo had started running as soon as Antonio had moved toward Chavez. He diverted his path when he saw Padilla drop the sword and begin drawing his pistol. There was just enough time for him to reach Markus, who was still rising, his back to Padilla.

Ricardo was drawing his own pistol, and put a hip into Markus, knocking him down again, and stepping between him and Padilla. Both men fired at the same time. And both men went down.

It might not be called a scream, but Morgana made a sound very similar to one, and rushed over to Ricardo. Elisabeth was beside Markus only a moment later, as he finally got to his feet.

His face was ashen. He looked over at Aislinn, saw that she was all right, helping Antonio. He went back to his knees beside Ricardo. Hernando was there a second later.

Morgana had Ricardo's head on her lap. "Ricardo!" she sobbed.

Markus' eyes widened slightly, but he put his attention back to his foreman and friend. There was blood on the side of Ricardo's head. Markus gently tried to move Ricardo's rather long hair out of the way to check the injury, but Ricardo groaned and opened his eyes. His right hand went to the side of his head.

Ricardo muttered a few low curses in Spanish, about Spaniards. Still sobbing, but now in relief, Morgana ran her hands over Ricardo's face. "Are you alright, Ricardo?" she asked gently.

It was obvious that Ricardo tried to nod, but changed his mind quickly as pain shot through his skull. "Yes, Señorita. I think so," he managed to say.

Markus had moved Ricardo's hair out of the way and could see the path of the ball that had grazed the side of Ricardo's head.

"I think he will be fine," Markus said. "It looks like a graze."

"His hard head saved him, I bet," his brother Hernando said, his love for his brother obvious in his husky voice, despite his words.

Looking between Morgana and Hernando, Markus decided Ricardo was in good hands. He rose and hurried over to Aislinn and Antonio. One of the men had ridden to get her medical bag and was handing it to her as Markus went to his knees once again, Elisabeth at his side.

"He stepped in front of Chavez," Aislinn said, rather calmly, Markus thought, despite the tears flowing down her face as she began to work on the wound in Antonio's hip.

When Antonio groaned loudly, Markus moved around and helped hold him still as Elisabeth helped Aislinn. Aislinn, as gently as she could, probed the wound and managed to remove the lead ball. She tossed it away and began to bandage the wound. Elisabeth had to help her finish, as Aislinn was shaking so much.

Aislinn's tears were copious now, and she was sobbing as she moved around to hold Antonio. It was a few moments, but Antonio's eyes opened. They were filled with pain, but there was much more there. And Markus could see it. And the similar look in Aislinn's eyes.

When Markus decided that Antonio was going to be fine for the moment with Aislinn, he rose and stepped away, Elisabeth again clutching his arm. He had recognized the looks in his sister's and Antonio's eyes, and those in Morgana's and Ricardo's eyes. They were the same as those in Elisabeth's eyes, and his own when he looked into a mirror.

With Ricardo and Hernando somewhat out of the picture, Agraciana had taken charge of the men. Agraciana was now third in command of the men, after Ricardo and Hernando. He and the men had disarmed Padilla and Chavez's soldiers. The workers that were to take the shipment to the coast had all disappeared early on. As they had been forced to be there, they had not been stopped by Ricardo and the men.

"Captain, what shall we do with Padilla's soldiers?"

"It's Markus," Markus insisted once again. He looked over at the cowed soldiers for a moment. Finally, he looked back at Agraciana. "Tell them they and the others have twelve hours to gather their personal things and leave the property and they will not be harmed. Not harmed by us. I make no promises as to what the other locals might do."

Markus looked at Ricardo, and Hernando helping Morgana with his brother, and then looked at Agraciana again. "Are you acceptable to taking the men to the property and supervising?"

"Yes, of course," Agraciana replied. "Ricardo and Hernando have been preparing me for additional duties for when we returned here. I am ready."

A corner of Markus' mouth turned up slightly. "I have full faith in you. Please see to it."

"Yes, Sir!" Agraciana replied enthusiastically. He moved off and began giving quiet, firm orders. Markus was pleased to see the men react well and do as requested.

Markus lent a hand as Antonio and Ricardo were readied to be taken to the estate. It was a slow process, though Markus thought it better both for the sake of the men, as well as to give Agraciana time to get things taken care of well before their arrival.

Elisabeth stayed right with him, within touching range most of the time. Markus did not mind. Aislinn might be the one that was fae, but Markus could feel, down to his very bones, that the future was a bright one for him, his soon to be wife, his sister, and all the others that had entered his life and been so much a part of it.

CHAPTER SEVEN

Present Day, Lynch Family Ocean Services Offices

Though there had not been much time to read on the last job, the one before that had allowed them to spend considerable time with the old journals, log book, and other documents they had recovered from Uncle Phil's house.

They were close to figuring out what had occurred, and as importantly, where, when the Irish Rose went down before starting that last job.

Working in their research workroom at the offices, it took only two days of concentrated research to make the breakthrough. Lee was on the computer, Cord with a dozen documents spread out on a table, when she gasped. "Cord! Look! I found it. I'm sure of it!"

Cord rolled his chair over and leaned forward, to look at the largest of the four monitors. Lee was using the mouse to circle a spot on a nautical chart.

"Here. You remember the inlet... cove... with the shoal that the Irish Rose hit? This matches. And look..." Lee scrolled the map slowly, so Cord could follow the course she was creating. "Here... This could be... probably is... where they camped..."

The Lee began to zoom back, until they could see and identify the area. Lee turned large green eyes toward Cord. His deep blue ones met hers. Cord whispered. "I think you found it."

Lee nodded. "What do we do? You know the laws..."

Cord smiled. "I think they will not be able to take it. With all this documentation, especially the pardons or whatever they were called then that resulted in there not being any charges brought, and full release to them of everything they had taken as pirates to compensate for the actions of the two rogue soldiers, we have provenance to prove ownership."

Lee's eyes widened. "You really think so? You know I do not mind giving up some of everything we do on our own to document things and have a visible history in museums and such. But the one hundred percent confiscation, plus having to pay for permits and such just does not sit well with me. I would rather not bring anything up if we only lose it all."

"I know, Lee," Cord replied. "You know I feel the same way. But this one is different." Cord looked thoughtful, staring at the far wall without seeing it.

He turned to Lee again. "We should talk to Reggie. Kind of give him a hypothetical situation. His knowledge of salvage law is even more extensive than Mom's is."

Cord noticed the slight pink that had appeared on Lee's face at the mention of Reginald Cooper. He decided the best course would be to ignore it.

Being a brother had certain responsibilities that he would not shirk. He would at least have to tease her a little bit, but subtly. He looked back at the computer monitor as he said, "Lee, you know this guy. You should be the one to lay out the scenario. You can make sure he addresses all of your concerns."

Cord looked back over at Lee. She was staring at him in alarm. She shook her head, and finally opened her mouth to protest.

Cord spoke first. "While you are doing that, I am going to go take a look at the Camille. See how close to ready for use she is after the refit."

With that Cord rose and strode toward the door of the workroom. As difficult as it was, he did not look back to see what Lee was doing.

Which was probably a good thing, as he would have caved and gone to see Reginald himself. Lee was staring toward the door, her mouth opening and closing soundlessly. Until she suddenly closed it, to capture the small scream she was making so no one could hear it.

Slapping the table slightly with a fist, Lee rose, muttering. "If he thinks I won't do it he is crazy. No way am I going to let that nose in the air, high faluten', overblown windbag get under my skin." Then in a whisper, "And after I get the information... then I will maim Cord."

Lee grabbed her jacket on the way out to get into her Cadillac XLR convertible to head for the Cooper, Cooper, and Henley Maritime Attorneys' offices.

Lee found herself muttering to herself and pressed her lips together tightly. She would not let Reginald get to her again. He was not worth it.

Suddenly she frowned. "Wait a minute. It's not that he is not worth it. It is that I am worth more to myself than allowing myself to let him affect me in any way."

Determined now that she was just fine, Lee finished the trip, taking care to avoid the worst of the drivers on the road. A storm was coming, and as usual, people were panicking, trying to get ready.

It was getting colder already, so when she parked, Lee put the Cadillac convertible's top up. It had been fine earlier, with the sun shining and the heater going, but not now.

After locking the car, Lee fastened her jacket and headed toward the entryway of the rather majestic building. There were many prestigious firms that had offices in the building, but, of course, Cooper, Cooper, and Henley had the whole top floor.

When Lee reached the entrance lobby reception desk, before she even opened her mouth, she heard Reginald call to her from the bank of elevators behind and to the side of the reception desk.

Lee looked over, to see Reginald standing there, looking at her. She noticed he still had one hand out to press the elevator call button, which seemed a bit strange. His hand came back to his side as he took a step toward her. "Lee! How nice to see you. How are you?"

Lee found herself a bit breathless. Reggie had always had that effect on her. She was sure it had faded, but perhaps not. She would not let it affect her right now, though. *I absolutely will not...*

"Hello, Reggie." Lee realized Reggie probably had not heard her, since she seemed to be whispering. She cleared her throat and tried again. "Hello, Reggie."

Finally getting her legs to work, she stepped forward, and managed to hold her hand out to shake Reggie's hand. *To keep it professional,* was the thought that crossed her mind.

"I am fine. Thank you for asking. And you?"

Lee saw Reggie's eyes flicker slightly. He took her hand, but she somehow forgot to shake it, and just held it instead as he looked into her eyes. She could not seem to look away.

"Good to hear. I am doing well."

Lee finally realized she was still holding his hand and quickly slipped it free. She cleared her throat again. "Are you headed out?" she asked. And almost winced when it occurred to her that she had just seen him reaching for the elevator call button. He was going in, not out.

"Actually, no. I'm headed up to my office. Can I direct you to a destination? Who are you here to see? I would be glad to walk you there."

"Um... I... Uh... actually came to talk to you..." She looked up and saw his eyes watching her. Hastily she added, "Professionally. Of course, professionally."

Reg simply nodded, "Of course. Well... Shall we go up, then?"

Lee nodded. They walked toward the elevator, Lee berating herself for not handling herself the way she intended. Reggie pressed the call button, and turned to face Lee as they waited. He said nothing, and Lee wanted to squirm.

"Are you sure you do not want Cord to handle this? Whatever 'this' is? You seem very uncomfortable. And I am sorry about that. I do not want to make you uncomfortable."

Lee's first reaction was that Reggie was still a very kind man, taking her feelings into account. Then the flash of anger hit. "I am quite capable of working with you on this. Do not flatter yourself that you have any effect on me at all."

Lee glared at Reggie as they stepped into the elevator. She thought she saw him start to smile. His eyes certainly showed a glint of humor. Lee was ready to say something, but the elevator chimed and the doors opened.

It caught Lee by surprise. "That elevator is fast," popped out before she could stop it.

Reggie chuckled. "That it is. Now, do you need some coffee or tea first? Or straight to business?"

"Business. Just business," Lee said, just a bit too loud. And much too plaintive.

"Very well," Reggie replied. He spoke to the receptionist as he led Lee toward his office. "Hold my calls, Louise. And reschedule Miss Hennessy for next Monday."

"She won't be happy," Louise responded, her eyes on Lee. Lee was sure that Louise had winked at her. "But I will take care of it."

Lee had turned toward the hallway she had gone down many times in the past. Reggie put a hand on her arm. "No. This way. I am in Dad's former office. I made partner early this year, and Dad retired."

"What?" Lee exclaimed. She stepped forward and her right hand went to Reggie's chest, her eye going to his. "That is wonderful, Reggie! You have worked so hard for that partnership! Congratulations! Why didn't you tell me?"

Suddenly Lee fell silent and stepped back, her hand leaving Reggie's chest. Her eyes went to the floor and a soft muttered, "Oh," left her lips.

Reggie had not said a word. His eyes were still on her when she lifted her eyes again. "Congratulations," Lee said again, quietly.

"Thank you, Lee," he replied. "It means a great deal to me." With a slight tilt of his head, he added, "This way."

Though Lee could tell that Reggie started to reach for her hand, the movement stopped as quickly as it had started. He took a step and Lee walked beside him, both of them silent.

Reggie opened the right-side door of the carved wooden double doors, and let Lee enter before him.

"My goodness!" Lee whispered. "This is magnificent!" She turned to look at Reggie. "You did all this?"

A half smile curled up Reggie's lips. "Not the doors, of course. But they were the inspiration for the rest. Which I did do myself."

Lee walked over to a bookcase. Every carved detail was easily visible under the beautiful finish that Reggie had applied. She moved on to the two matching credenzas, the base cabinets, upper cabinets, a hutch, armoire and more book cases.

More cabinetry in the sitting area as well as heavy wood and leather seating, the furniture also with intricate carving. As were the end tables and coffee table.

Lee turned back around. And finally looked at the desk, which she had intentionally left for last.

"Oh, my word... Reggie..."

She finally turned to look at him. "It is magnificent! Just as you used to describe it." Her eyes went back to the desk. And then the chair. She did a double take. It was a nice chair, but...

When she looked back toward Reg he smiled. "I am adding a few things to the chair. It was not quite ready when I got the partnership."

"Oh..." Lee looked around the office again. "You really have done it, Reggie. Partner... Your dream office..."

She looked over at him. "I am so proud of you. Your mother would be ecstatic."

A sad smile was on his face, but gone in an instant. "Yes... I do like to think so."

He motioned to one of the chairs in front of the desk, and then took the chair behind it. As he settled himself, and Lee did the same, touching the wood and leather of the chair for a moment, Reggie quietly said, "You do know that you are what inspired all this? Don't you?"

Lee cut wide eyes up to Reggie's. "What? No. I guess I did not hear you correctly."

Reg could tell Lee was not ready to talk about 'them'. Her and him. As a couple, but she would be. He smiled and dropped that conversation.

"Now. What is it that brought you to Cooper, Cooper, and Henley, Maritime Attorneys?"

Lee inhaled, held the breath for a moment and then let it out in a soft sigh.

"You and the company are still on the books as clients, on retainer. So anything said will be covered under client attorney privileged confidentiality. Nothing will go anywhere you do not want it to go, Lee. I hope you know that you can trust me."

Lee nodded slightly, realizing that she did trust him, despite their personal relationship problems. "I know, Reggie. Cord and I trust you. We do anyway, and this... situation... will require it. This is really important to Cord and me. And to the entire family. It has to do with our history, as well as the potential of acquiring a huge amount of money."

"I see," Reginald replied, watching Lee. He leaned back in the chair slightly, and clasped his hands just below his chest. "This sounds intriguing." He did sit up straight when a thought came to him. "Lee, you are aware... I think I mentioned it... but I'm not sure..."

Lee looked at him curiously. Reggie never showed doubt.

"I... You are aware that we are related... from way, way back... Not in any way recently. I never would have... Well, it is far beyond... like even fourth cousins three times removed or something." Reginald paused for a moment, and before Lee could respond, added, "A common ancestor. That is what it is. We have a common ancestor."

"We do?" Lee asked, not even all that surprised at what Reggie said. The family had branches all over the area, many of them intertwined with each other. All from that first group with Markus and Aislinn Lynch. "Who?" Lee asked.

"Aislinn Lynch. Through Antonio Montebon's side of the family. Aislinn's husband."

"Oh... Markus' sister. We are through Markus..."

"Yes," Reginald replied. "I know. I really thought I had mentioned it."

"No," Lee said. "I don't remember, anyway. But it doesn't matter... well about..." She fell silent for a moment, but quickly continued. "About this..."

Again, she paused and looked thoughtful. Reginald stayed silent and let her think.

"Actually, this may matter." She looked back at Reginald. "You are part of the family. So it will affect you..."

"Perhaps you should tell me what this is all about..." Reginald replied, now sitting with his forearms on the desk, leaning forward slightly, intent on Lee.

Lee had to catch her breath. Reggie looked so... She shook her head just slightly, looked at Reggie again, and began to speak.

As always, Lee noted, Reggie concentrated on what she was saying, taking copious notes and only interrupting for specific clarification. When she had finished, she watched as Reggie sat back, and much like hers was earlier, his stare was far away as he thought.

Then his eyes snapped back to meet Lee's. Quietly he told her, "This is big, Lee. Very big. The history... the money... even if secondary, will be big, if what I have learned and am beginning to believe, is true."

"What about provenance? Do you think we will be able to maintain control of everything?" Lee saw the small smile start to form on Reggie's face, and felt one forming on hers.

"I believe so, Lee. I will do the due diligence research to make sure. But with the log books, the diaries, and journals, added to the birth records which I know your family has, as well as my family's records that have been kept, even from well before Aislinn and Antonio met and married."

Closing her eyes, and saying a short but heartfelt prayer, Lee relaxed just a bit more. She stood after opening her eyes, to find Reginald had moved from behind the desk and was now within arm's reach. A tiny "Oh!" escaped her lips.

"Sorry," Reginald muttered, taking a step back.

Lee, before she could stop herself, reached out to place a hand on his arm. "It's okay, Reggie. Just caught me by surprise."

The slight electrical charge that seemed to pass between them at the point of touch had Lee taking a step back, and then another, her eyes on Reggie's.

"I... Um... Better get going," Lee said, after finally drawing another breath into her lungs. "Cord will want to know it looks like the project is good to go."

"I'll walk you down," Reginald said, in a voice that Lee knew meant he would not be talked out of it.

Lee nodded and headed for the door. Reggie, of course, was there first, with those long legs of his, and she had to step past him to go through. She made sure not to breathe in his scent, which was something she used to love to do.

She managed to engage in a bit of small talk with Reggie on the way down the elevator about some mutual acquaintances. And then they were walking past the reception desk on the first floor, toward the outer doors.

"Lee," Reginald said, "You said the project could go forward. I take it that means you will be raising some things..."

Despite Reginald's very low voice, with a quick touch of hand on arm again, Lee as much as whispered, "Not in public, Reggie. Too big of a risk."

The small smile that appeared on Reginald's face was more for the fact that her words gave him an even better opportunity than he was hoping for by bringing up his involvement on the project now.

"Of course, Lee. I quite understand. I will be much more careful in the future. So, in keeping with the need to stay under the radar, I will meet you at the new place tomorrow. Say about seven? I will see you then."

Before Lee could protest, Reginald had spun on his heel and was walking rapidly toward the elevator. She almost ran after him to protest, but changed her mind instantly. A small smile formed, despite her attempt to make herself frown for his audacity.

She was back in her office when Cord returned. She looked up when he gave a soft knock on the frame of the open door. "Hey, Sis. What did Reggie have to say?"

"He was pretty sure that the provenance would hold up. But he is going to do some due diligence research in addition to what he already knows."

Lee hesitated a moment, but met Cord's eyes again. "I was pretty open with him about what might be down there. And did you know he has a common ancestor with us? His family is from Antonio Montero's side of the family."

"Yep. I remember him mentioning that. A long time ago. But he is willing to help us?"

Lee nodded. "Yes." Then she frowned. "And has invited himself to a meeting tomorrow at the new place at seven."

Cord noted the frown on Lee's face. "Invited himself? I am surprised you mentioned it."

Lee looked surprised. "Actually, now that I think about it, I did not mention the new place or anything about having any meetings there." Lee shook her head. "I don't know how he does some of that."

"You trust him, Lee? After what... Whatever he did?"

Lee seemed to have been lost in thought, but her eyes snapped back to meet Cords. "Of course I do! Reggie can be trusted. He and I just... Never mind. You... We... Can depend on him."

Cord managed not to grin before he turned away from Lee. "A bit too adamant there, he thought. "We shall see what we shall see.

Later, after the others had left, Cord and Lee continued to work. Both worked on different sections of the still tentative plan. Primarily the initial logistics of getting ready to go on a salvage operation with somewhat limited information available.

Lee seemed distracted the next day. Cord decided to give her some space to perhaps work on how she might work things out with Reggie. Hopefully.

Cord shook his head. Reggie called or would run into Cord from time to time, and always asked about Lee, first, before whatever it was he said he needed to talk to Cord about. Cord decided early on that Reggie simply wanted to know that Lee was all right. Everything else was just idle chat.

At four Cord decided to call it a day at the office, and headed over to the new boat and ship service, maintenance, repair, and customization shop building that Lynch Family Ocean Services now owned and operated.

It was where the Camille was being brought back to life after being abandoned for years. After basic repairs and modernization work, she would be set up and equipped as a research and exploration vessel, while still having full provisions for use as a recovery tug and search and salvage ship for the company when not being used for research and exploration.

He was wondering where Lee had disappeared to just before he had decided to leave early himself. Cord shook his head. She would show up for the meeting, he was sure.

Deeply involved in the installation of some deck equipment on the Camille, Cord started slightly when Lee touched his shoulder and called his name again.

"Cord!" Lee said fairly loudly. "I've called for you three times. Are you okay?"

Cord stood up and turned around. "Yes. I'm fine. I was just concentrating on the work, I guess. This equipment has to be installed properly for safety."

"You were thinking about the salvage the other day..."

Cord started to shake his head, and had opened his mouth to deny Lee's statement, but realized that perhaps it had been in the back of his mind.

"You could be right, Lee," he admitted. "That wreck, I guess it did get to me a bit more than I thought."

Lee nodded in understanding. "Yeah. Same here." To change the subject, Lee asked Cord, "So, how is this work going? I can see quite a few additions have been done."

Glad to be away from the other subject, and always willing to talk ships, Cord began to explain what had been accomplished and what was left to be done.

Lee was well schooled in maritime construction, though it was not her specialty, the way it was Cord, but she always wanted to know everything about the business.

When they came back onto the deck after being down in the engine room, Lee's steps faulted slightly when she saw Reggie standing just inside the door of the cavernous main work area of the building.

Cord noticed the stumble, but said nothing about it as Lee preceded him from the deck of the Camille to the floor of the building. He did say, "What is that he is carrying?" when Reggie picked up something and started forward to meet them.

"Looks like an engineering portfolio... or something." Lee replied.

Reggie set the large leather case down and shook Cord's hand. "Cord."

"Hey, Reggie."

"Lee," Reggie said, his eyes going to hers.

"Umm... Yes... Well, I suppose we should go into the offices..."

Reggie cut his eyes from her, several moments after she had turned and started toward the wall dividing the large work area from the other specialty shops the building contained, as well as the offices.

Reggie colored slightly when he looked at Cord again, and found Cord watching him. "I... Ah..."

Softly, Cord said, "It is okay, Reggie. I know you... Never mind. Between you two. But... Just be careful, okay? For her and for yourself."

Reggie nodded. "Yes. Thanks, Cord."

The two hurried to catch up with Lee. As they neared the door they would go through, Reggie was asking Cord, "Any chance of a tour before I leave? I sure would like to see what you've done with the old girl. She has an amazing history."

"That she does," Cord agreed. "Sure. Should be plenty of time, unless you have a meeting to attend. Or a date, later."

Reggie and Lee both glared at him for a moment, but after glancing at each other, both decided it better not to acknowledge the dig from Cord. Both knew it was directed at both of them to elicit some kind of reaction.

"I'll give you a reaction..." Lee muttered. Cord grinned, and Reggie looked a bit uncertain.

"We were wondering what you brought with you," Cord said, changing the subject. He had made his point.

"Oh this." Reggie nodded to the leather case in his hand. "Yes. I think you will find some of it interesting. I'd rather wait until I can lay everything out. It'll be easier to explain that way."

"You'll have your chance in just a few minutes," Lee said, opening the door to a large conference room. "I'll get us some coffee and some water, if you want to set up."

"And I need to hit the head," Cord added, not even entering the room.

"Okay. It will only take a couple of minutes. And I see the audio-visual gear over there. That will work great."

Lee did not exactly frown, but her nose wrinkled slightly, Reggie noticed, and her eyes squinted a bit in curiosity.

"You need A/V equipment?" Lee shook her head. "Never mind. I 'll be back in a few minutes."

Cord and Reg were standing at the far end of the large table, with the A/V cart within reach when Lee pushed the refreshment cart inside.

She parked it against the wall behind the A/V cart. "Water, coffee, things for tea." She took a bottle of water and took a chair on the other side of the table.

Cord got his necessary coffee, and Reggie prepared his cuppa. He noted that there were several bags of his favorite tea, Bigelow Earl Grey, along with a few more tea options.

"If you are ready," Cord said, "I'll make the call and get the conference call started."

Reggie nodded. After Lee looked at Reg for a moment, she also nodded. "Let's see how this goes."

Cord set up the phone for the conference call and then hit the first of the speed dial buttons. As each of the lines connected Cord made introductions as necessary. When everyone was connected, Cord began to explain the reason for the call.

"You know that Lee and I closed Uncle Phillip's estate a few months ago. Everything was handled according to his will of course. But there were a few things found in his family history files that were... to put it mildly, rather surprising."

Cord went on to explain the discovery of the journals, maps, and charts, along with the artifacts from the Irish Rose.

"Wait a minute," broke in their cousin Francis. "Are you saying that Markus and Aislinn were pirates? And Morgana, too? I don't believe it. They were farmers and horse breeders."

Cord looked over at Lee with a plea in his eyes. Cousin Francis was always difficult to deal with. Since she was a descendant of Morgana and Ricardo Estrada, not Markus or Aislinn, there tended to be some friction at times in the last three generations. They were all considered family, but more extended family than immediate.

"Cousin Francis," Lee said, her voice calm, "there have always been the rumors about something in the families' past that has mostly just been considered that, rumors.

"But what we found pretty much confirms not only that there was something, but exactly what. I am working on putting an organized timeline and history together to send to everyone, with copies of the documentation.

"But for the moment, the Irish Rose is the primary concern of this meeting. Cord and I believe we should try to recover what we can of the ship and anything it contained as soon as we can.

"It certainly is not common knowledge, but people are always looking for old Spanish treasure Galleons along the coast. If someone runs across the Irish Rose simply by chance, the families could lose control of it, with little likelihood of regaining control afterward.

"There is the possibility of some treasure," Lee said. Cord gave her a quick look, but she went on.

"But it isn't our main concern. There is not much, if any, record of Markus and Aislinn having done anything other than start the farm and ranch, and then start the timber operation and the sawmill and maritime support services. That has always been considered their sources of income.

"Very similar to what we do now, since that original business has been handed down the family line since Markus' death and then Aislinn's.

"If this all turns out to be true, and I think it is, then the history should be made known, and what happened back then revealed. Having read the journals and other documentation, I can tell you, it sounds like a very remarkable history."

When Lee stopped talking, Francis did not respond. Ralph Jenkins, another cousin through a distant common ancestor asked, "How much is this going to cost us? How much would the treasure be worth? And can we keep it hidden from the government? I know they consider everything found in territorial waters theirs, and even outside territorial waters most of the time too."

Lee looked over at Cord. She could tell he was annoyed at the questions. And the attitude. It seemed that family and family history did not mean the same, or as much, to some as it did to him, Lee, and some of the others they were closer to, even if more remotely related.

"Tell you what," Cord said. Lee winced.

Reggie saw the look on Lee's face, and the annoyance on Cord's as Cord continued to speak.

"Yeah. I tell you what. Lee and I will cover the cost of the recovery. It will not cost the extended family anything. But in so doing, we will consider everything we find, that we are allowed to keep, ours to do with as we wish. Keep it ourselves, sell it, donate or sell to museums, give parts to the different family lines.

"Pretty much whatever we want. It is going to cost several million dollars to do this, unless everything goes absolutely perfectly and the ship is not as deep as we think, and no one finds it before we do and can stake our claim."

"I don't know," said Cousin Marjorie. "That doesn't sound fair. To y'all, I mean. Honey, that could bankrupt you if there isn't anything there, couldn't it? I'd hate to see you throw away one of the family's business on a whim or wild goose chase."

Cord was glaring at the phone. Lee looked stricken. Reggie made a snap decision. "Cooper, Cooper, and Henley will underwrite the expedition. We will provide insurance to ensure the Lynch family business will not be endangered."

Reggie cut a glance at Lee and then Cord. Ignoring both the amazement at his words, and the gestures and indicators that they would not accept his offer, Reggie added, "But this is dependent on it being through the current Lynch Services business, with them being the sole authority and owner of anything resulting from the expedition, with Cooper, Cooper, and Henley taking a small, to be agreed upon fee for the service."

He could tell both Cord and Lee were going to protest, but he held up both hands, one toward each of them, and nodded to the phone.

Several people were talking at once. After a few moments everyone shut up, and then began speaking one at a time.

"I say we let them take the risk. OUR side of the family were not pirates, and I do not want them, or me, connected to this in any way. Do what you want. But do not involve our name in this farce. We will sue, if you do. And that is no conjecture. It is a fact. Good-bye."

There was the sound of one line going off-line. Lee and Cord stared at each other as most of the rest on the call said basically the same thing. Some more politely, some with simple one sentence declines, but all with an admonishment not to attach their family names with any part of the venture, most especially any mention of pirates in the family tree.

Finally, there were two lines still active. "Lee, you still there, sweetie?"

"Yes, Aunt Maggie." Lee's voice was low, her disappointment obvious.

"Well, Honey, you can count on me. I have always thought the rumors were probably true. Nothing wrong with having a horse thief or pirate, in the family line. Pretty much every family does, somewhere back there. Probably what keeps some family lines vigorous. Those kinds of genes are strong ones.

"You know I don't have much money now, but any moral support I can give, you know you only have to ask. And I do not expect or want anything in return. Except the story, when you have it all."

"Thank you, Aunt Maggie," Lee said.

"Yes," Cord said, adding his thanks. "And you can consider yourself an investor. We both appreciate your support and belief in the project."

"No need, little Cord. But appreciated. We can discuss all that after you come back with the proof of our ancestors' great accomplishments." The line went dead before Lee or Cord could respond.

The last phone line indicator was still lit. Neither Lee or Cord were sure who was on that line.

And they still did not have a clue after a male voice spoke, with a woman's laughter in the background. "You are so clueless..." And then he laughed. The line went dead.

Lee, Cord, and Reggie exchanged startled glances.

"Who was that?" Lee asked.

"I don't know," Cord responded.

Brother and sister looked at Reggie. Reggie shook his head. "I hope you don't think I..."

"No," Lee said adamantly. "I've already told Cord I trust you. Completely. We know you had nothing to do with anything in that phone call."

Lee continued to look at Reggie for a moment, but she could not wait any longer. "Why, Reggie? Why did you offer to underwrite us? We won't let you, of course, and you know it. But why did you offer?"

"It is a real offer," Reggie said quietly, looking at Lee, without a glance at Cord. "And because I believe. I have researched the family for years. Mostly my line back, but it is all connected, so I found records about things..." He shook his head.

"It is real. And not only am I curious, I want to help. Because it is a risk for you. And now... That last voice... That has me worried. I do not want anything to happen to you. Either of you. Or your business."

Reggie did look over at Cord then. He found Cord watching him thoughtfully. Then Cord looked at Lee a moment but still did not say anything, but Reggie was sure he saw Cord give a slight nod.

Looking back at Lee, Reggie said, "I want to go with you on the expedition." He could see Lee start to protest, but continued quickly. "I think when you see what I have here, and explain a couple of more things I intended to bring up, anyway, that you will see that I can be of assistance. And the offer to underwrite any or all of the cost still stands."

Before Lee could speak, Cord did, bringing quick looks to him from both of the others. "Fifteen percent."

"Done," Reggie said.

"Wait a minute!" Lee protested, standing up angrily. "You can't just give him fifteen percent of our business. And I am not convinced he'd be of any help on the trip, anyway." Lee glared at Reggie for a moment, but turned back to Cord when she spoke again. "If anything, he will be in the way. A problem any way you look at it."

Hands on her hips, she looked from Cord to Reggie and back.

"Please look this over," Reggie said calmly as he stood and made a sweeping motion across the things he had arranged on the table.

"I need a pit stop, and then I will be back to discuss this."

A frown and another glare from Lee followed Reggie out of the room.

She looked around at Cord when he stood and began to pick up and look at each of the papers and other objects that Reggie had brought. Lee saw his eyes widen. She took the paper Cord handed over to her.

Lee's eyes widened as well. It was a diving certification. Cord handed her three more. And then several other certifications for various maritime jobs and activities.

When Reggie returned, having taken as much time as he could stand, he found Cord standing, looking at the A/V materials one-by-one.

It was Lee, however, whom Reggie first looked. She was facing the large monitor but leaning back in one of the chairs. When he could see the side of her face, she looked defeated. Which was not what he had wanted at all.

"You are in," she said when she saw him out of the corner of her eyes. She did not look at him as she added, "Fifteen percent. Your documents, or copies, go with anything we find."

Lee spun the chair around, the way away from Reggie. "The Camille will be ready at the end of the month. Be prepared to be gone a minimum of two months, up to as much as three."

With that she walked toward the door of the conference room. Reggie had not said a word. He had no idea what to say. When he turned, he saw Cord watching him.

Cord opened his mouth, but closed it without speaking. He helped Reggie gather up and put away the papers and other items into the leather case.

As they walked toward their respective vehicles, Cord paused, looked at Reggie and said only, "You have your work cut out for you."

Cord got in his truck and drove away, Reggie watching for a moment before he got in his rig and went home. He decided to put the documents back in the safe when he got home, not wanting to leave them out in the humidity that had climbed as a front came through.

It was then that he saw one of the papers as he put them back in order by size and shape. "Oh," he sighed. "No wonder... How could I have left that with these?"

Reggie almost crumbled up the document to hurl it across the room, but he controlled himself tightly. He needed to hang onto it, just in case Dawn went back on her agreement.

With a sigh, Reggie turned and went over to the safe, opened it and put the document away. As he closed and locked the safe, his thoughts drifted back to the time that all that had happened.

He and Lee were having lunch at one of the marina restaurants when a woman walked up to their table and spoke to Lee. "You, huh. Did he tell you about me? The soon to be mother to his child?"

Lee saw Reggie's jaw drop down in shock. "What are you talking about?" Reggie asked. Lee trusted Reggie implicitly. She would let him handle whatever this was.

This time the woman nearly screamed. "You don't even remember? You don't remember me? Las Vegas. Last fall at the convention?" The woman had pulled out her phone, touched the screen a couple of times and thrust it toward, not to Reggie, but Lee. "This bring it back to you, big time lawyer?"

Lee saw the picture of Reggie in a casino, with a woman slightly behind him and to one side. It was Dawn, Lee was sure. She arched her eyebrows slightly, looking over at Reggie. She felt no reason to mistrust him. He would have an explanation.

"Why don't I go powder my nose while you work this out. Meet me at the entrance when you are ready, Reggie."

Reggie reached over and gently, thought Lee, turned the phone toward him. When Lee saw the recognition on Reggie's face, his softly said, "Oh...", and then his quick look over at her, Lee, not even a quarter up out of her chair, sat back down, a questioning look on her face. More curiosity than anything. She had tried to tease Reggie over the years, and he was unflappable. Anything that got that kind of reaction out him was noteworthy.

The woman, seeing that Lee did not seem upset turned back to Reggie as he rose from his chair. "Go outside Dawn. I will be there sho..."

"You do remember now, don't you, Mr. Lawyer Man." She glanced over at Lee. "Trust him, don't you? Well, listen to this."

Dawn turned back to Reggie. Lee could tell that Reggie wanted to take Dawn's arm to escort her out of the restaurant, as people were now looking toward them.

Lee knew Reggie would not. He was too much a gentleman to manhandle a woman. And it was clear it would take manhandling to get Dawn to move.

"Did you not ask me to go to your room? Me, a 'working girl'?" Dawn winked at Lee over the term 'working girl'.

Lee saw the agony in Reggie's eyes. She had her first glimmering of doubt when he barely whispered, "Yes."

"Did you not take me up to your room, with my dress half off?"

Reggie stood mute. Not denying it, Lee noted.

"Did you not strip me and put me in your bed?"

Agonized eyes went to Lee. Still with no denials. Lee felt a chill go down her back. She felt her resolve to let Reggie have the benefit of the doubt begin to leave her.

"Did you not pay me off the next morning, get me a cab, and send me away, with barely a word?"

"And have you ever sent me any money to help out with the pregnancy and birth of your baby and help with taking care of him?"

Lee saw Reggie react slightly to the last question, but she just could not stay any longer. "I will let you sort this out..." Lee's words were strangled.

"Lee..." Reggie said, his plea fading as she hurried away.

Reggie turned to Dawn. "What is this all about?" Dawn could hear the controlled anger in his voice, but she was not worried. He was a big shot, with much to lose, and everyone said he never got physical. About anything.

"Outside!" he growled. He started to reach for her arm again. She laughed at him when he clenched his fist and put it down at his side. Tossing some money on the table, Reggie strode off toward the front door of the restaurant.

Dawn almost reached for the money on the table, but a server was headed that way, and she decided she would have enough in a little while so followed Reggie, at a slow, strutting stroll.

"What are you trying to do?" Reggie asked, spinning on his heel as soon as they were both outside and in a spot that was not too visible. "You know perfectly well that nothing happened. I just tried to keep you from getting into trouble with the casino for soliciting. You were too drunk to do anything remotely logical. I just tried to help you."

"Yeah. Well, sweetie, I am in need of a bit more help now. And you are just the man to provide it." Her voice had a hard edge to it now. "I need twenty grand to get rid of the tyke, and another thirty to get somewhere safe. Fifty kay is nothing to you. Hand it over and I will be out of your hair forever."

"A tyke? You mean a baby? We didn't do anything. It certainly is not my baby."

"No, you idiot. It is my last boyfriend's baby. He's in the mob and he found out I had a baby. I didn't know about the baby until after I split from him after a rich Texan offered me a much better opportunity.

"Tex would not hear of me getting rid of it. So I had to have it. And now Tex is dead, and I'm stuck with the kid, 'cause it turns out he never got around to changing his will. His ex and kids get it all and I get nothing. I had that kid because of him..."

Reggie could not believe Dawn's callousness. No care or concern about her own child. It made him physically ill. And before he even considered anything else at all, he promised himself to make sure that child was rescued from his mother, and if possible, kept from his mob boss father.

Pulling out one of his cards, Reggie wrote an address and phone number on the back. He gave it to Dawn, rather forcefully, and said, "Be there tomorrow at noon. And bring the child. And everything of his."

With that, Reggie stalked off, without a backward glance.

Dawn smiled, tucked the card away, and walked over to an old Cadillac on its last legs. A babies' eyes followed her from a child carrier in the back seat. "Well, kid, you won't be a burden on me for much longer."

With a laugh, Dawn ground the starter of the Caddy until if finally started.

Though Dawn resisted, when Reggie looked like he was going to walk away, she signed the document that Reggie had prepared the night before. She signed three copies, actually. Two for Reggie and one for her.

And Reggie made sure she understood the consequences if she violated any part of the provisions in the document.

When Dawn drove away, Reggie stood there with a baby in his arms, a child carrier and one Walmart cloth shopping bag at his feet. The baby suddenly gurgled a bit, and Reggie felt moisture on his left arm.

"I guess I better get you to your new home, little one." It was only at that moment that Reggie realized that Dawn had not uttered the baby's name one time.

When Reggie got the baby to the child services offices, he went through everything with the agent. There was not a single identifying thing in the lot.

Reggie gave the woman a copy, not an original, of the document. Along with a check, and another document giving the details of a trust fund he had set up for the child. After one last look at the little baby boy, Reggie hardened his heart, turned and walked away.

With the hope that Lee would give him a chance to explain, since she was the most understanding and compassionate woman he knew, he went to see her.

And she probably would have, Reggie was sure, except, before she left town, Dawn made a point to ambush Lee in the parking lot of the Lynches' business, in order to tell her that Reggie had come through on his parental duties as she waved the wad of cash in her hands.

When Reggie tried to contact her, she would not take his calls, respond to voice mail, e-mail, regular mail, and would walk away if she saw him out in public.

Again, Reggie shook his head. He gathered up the rest of the documents, stacked them together, and put them away. The one thing that brought a slight smile to his face was that now, perhaps, on this trip, he would have the chance, and Lee would be open to him explaining what the truth was.

This time, he would say the words he had intended to say that day. Reggie touched the ring box in his center drawer of his desk in the study as he put away the paper clips that he had stripped off the documents.

Chapter 8

The time passed quickly. The Camille was ready as scheduled, with a successful sea trial and test of all the new equipment. She was fully fueled and stocked with provisions and supplies. Early on the Sunday morning they had agreed upon, Lee drove into the parking lot at the docks where the ship was berthed.

As she was unloading her personal gear from her Suburban, Cord drove up and began to unload his from his Ram. Seconds later Reggie was on the other side of Lee's rig, doing the same thing. After greeting each other, and Lee and Cord accepted the take-out cups that Reggie offered, with thanks they finished their unloading and organizing.

No sooner had Reggie and Cord returned with a dolly for their ditch bags, duffel bags, and computer and instrument cases than the rest of the employees that would be crewing the ship arrived in one of the company transport vans.

Four men and three women, laughing and joking with each other, piled out of the van and began to unload it after exchanging good mornings. One went after another dolly. In less than an hour, everything was aboard the Camille, stowed and ready. A final inspection by Cord and it was time to go, just as the sun was fully above the horizon.

With Lee at the helm, Cord and Reggie overseeing the deck crew, the moorings were released and retrieved and the ship pushed away from the dock a few inches as the engines idled.

Lee engaged the drives, and they idled away from the dock. It was a no-wake area, so Lee barely nudged the throttles to make way toward the outlet to the Atlantic.

Once clear of the no-wake zone, Lee sounded the maneuvering warning, and after a few moments pushed the throttles forward slowly.

A few minutes later Cord and Reggie joined her on the bridge. "Maggie'll have breakfast ready shortly," Cord told Lee.

Lee nodded. "Take the helm? That tea seemed to have gone right through me."

"Sure," Cord replied. He looked over at Reggie. "You up to some refresher training?"

Reggie rolled his eyes and Lee laughed. It was like old times. Almost. She hurried down into the ship to use the head as Reggie took the wheel in her place. They were off to see if they could recover the treasure from their ancestors' pirating days.

After everyone had a chance to have breakfast, Lee, Cord and Reggie were on the bridge. Lee was at the helm again. The three were discussing the possibilities of what they might run into at the dive site. They had obtained the latest charts for the area and Reggie had obtained some very old maps and charts, dating from the early 1700s onward, to add to those that he already had and those that were in the papers that Lee and Cord had found at their uncle's place.

They were still travelling due east, to get well away from the coast before turning south, just as a precaution. All three suddenly stared at the Marine VHF radio mounted in the console. As required by law, the radio was set to monitor the Marine VHF emergency and calling channel, Channel 16.

Channel 16 was the channel ships and boats used to make initial contact with another ship or boat, whereupon they would switch to another frequency for their conversation.

They had been hearing the occasional call between other ships, but this call was for the Camille. Lee reached for the mike and answered. "This is the Camille."

"It's Gilmore, Lee. I have a passenger that wants to board."

"What?" Lee asked. She looked over at Cord and Reggie.

"She says she is Reginald's sister and needs to see him."

Cord and especially Lee, gave a sharp look at Reggie.

"You don't have a sister," Cord said, just as Reggie spoke.

"I don't have a sister."

Lee's eyes narrowed when she saw the sudden understanding in Reggie's demeanor, and his muttered, "Oh. Magdalena."

"Another one?" Lee let slip out. And it came out rather more loudly than she would ever have thought she would speak, if she had even thought she would say it out loud.

Reggie saw her frown and turn away from him to look forward through the windshield. Her back stiff, she set the mike where Reggie could reach it and moved as far from that point as she could and still have good control of the wheel.

Reggie picked up the mike and keyed it. "Magdalena, what do you want? How did you even find out where I am?"

Reggie winced when Lee snorted slightly.

"Come on, bro," came a woman's voice over the radio.

Keying the mic again, Reggie told Gilmore to switch to another channel to get off the calling and emergency channel. After Gilmore acknowledged, Reggie reached over, Lee leaning way back to avoid any contact and changed the radio to the new channel.

"Magdalena, what are you doing out here?"

"I need to talk to you, bro. It's important."

"Now?"

"Yes. It's about... Well, you know. What you guys are doing."

Lee and Cord exchanged startled and worried glances.

"Let's get her on board before she says something we don't want known," Cord said.

Lee frowned, but she did not say anything.

With a sigh, Reggie told Gilmore to get ready for the transfer.

Reluctantly, Lee throttled back the Camille, allowing it to lose way, and turned into the slight breeze to help keep things stable.

Reggie and Cord went out on deck to handle the transfer. The water was too rough for the two craft to come to a complete stop, so they would maintain a bit of way, which would help stabilize them more than stopping would.

Gilmore edged the Mary Lou over closer to the Camille once he matched her speed. Both ships had fenders out, so when they bumped slightly as a wave shifted the Mary Lou a bit more than Gilmore wanted there was no damage.

Reggie and Cord reached out, each grabbing one of the woman's hands. She simply stepped from the railing of the Mary Lou to the railing of the Camille, and then down onto the deck without a bobble.

Gilmore waved from the bridge of the Mary Lou and eased her away from the Camille before running up the throttles to make the turn to head back to shore.

With Reggie and Cord both having a firm grip on the woman's arm, the three went back to the bridge. Magdalena flipped back the hood of the light jacket she was wearing against the chill in the air and misting rain that kept trying to form. That was when Cord got his first real look at her. He had been concentrating on getting her aboard safely, and between that and the hood, he had not got a good look at her face. Or body.

Lee looked back and managed to not gasp when Magdalena slipped out of the jacket and she got a good look at her. It was a slightly different reaction than Cord's, but just as strong.

Magdalena was a real beauty. Model quality beauty, Lee decided. Not runway model beauty, but slim, trim, athletic model beauty. Lee cut her eyes to Reggie, but the wheel in her hand was reacting to the water and she had to look forward.

Cord, on the other hand, could not stop looking at her. Even as Reggie led her over to the chart room, he almost followed. Lee cleared her throat when she turned again and saw him.

"Oh..." Cord said at the look Lee gave him. "I guess they need to talk privately..."

"No doubt," Lee replied.

Cord could hear both disappointment and just a touch of annoyance in her voice. He decided he might just have a word with Reggie, despite having decided to stay out of whatever was going on between him and Lee. He did not like seeing her beginning to hurt the way she did before.

Although they had not slid the panel door closed, and Cord and Lee could hear the murmur of their voices, they could not understand them. Cord was checking the ships system instrumentation, just to get a good feeling for the ship while it was underway with a standard load, just for something to do.

After only a few minutes, Lee was beginning to wonder a bit about what was going on with Reggie and Magdalena, as the murmuring did not seem to be either angry or even controversial. Nor, she felt, did it seem anything... romantic. She was simply not sure what was going on. She was about to find out, as was Cord.

Lee turned to take a look when she heard Reggie say, "You two need to hear this. Magdalena has some information that may change what we do and how we do it."

Lee and Cord exchanged a look, communicated silently, as brother and sisters often do, and Cord used the intercom to call one of the crew up to take the wheel.

When Lee was relieved at the helm, she and Cord led the way to the dining area by the ship's galley. With coffee or tea in hand, the four took seats at one of the tables.

"Magdalena, though I introduced her as my sister," said Reggie, "is not my sister by blood. But she is like a sister to me. Has been since we were small. When her parents were killed in a car accident when she was six, Mom and Dad took her in since her parents were close friends. She stayed with us for a couple of years until her aunt, who was young herself, was in a position to take care of her. But we have stayed close."

Reggie made the introductions again, with less tension involved. That done, Reggie turned to Magdalena and said, "Tell them what you told me."

Magdalena looked at Cord and then Lee. If she noticed Cord's interest in her that was far beyond anything she might say, she did not give any indication.

She cut her eyes over to Reggie for a moment before looking back to Lee. "Although Reggie was never happy with my choice, I was going out with a guy... A real jerk it turns out. I broke it off quite a while ago, but we frequent many of the same places, attend many of the same events, have the occasional business interaction.

"I overheard him mention his ex-wife once, not long after I first went out with him. The name sounded familiar. The last name anyway. I never really thought about it after that until recently. He and his..." Magdalena rolled her eyes. "Girlfriend of the moment, were at a presentation dinner I attended as a presenter. He came in just after I had made my presentation and was on the way back to my table.

"I do not think he realized that I was seated at a table behind where he was. I was close enough to hear him whispering to two other people during a lull in the activities. One of the people was the girlfriend. But the other one I did not know, other than he was in some type of maritime business. I really was trying to ignore the conversation, which should have been easy since they were whispering.

"I guess as the noise level increased, so did their voices so they could hear each other, even though they were still talking softly. So I was able to hear Kennedy mention his ex-wife's name again. And this time I remembered from where I knew the name."

Magdalena looked at Reggie for a moment and added. "It was your great grandmother's name."

Reggie looked at Cord and then at Lee. "Grandmother Elisa Montebon," he explained.

"Montebon! That was Aislinn's husband's name. You said you are related to us through him," Lee exclaimed.

Reggie nodded. All three of the others looked at Magdalena again. She nodded. "I probably would not have thought all that much about it since it was his ex-wife's maiden name. But when he mentioned something about getting to something before Reggie and, I quote, 'the others', it caught my interest for sure. I started listening a bit more closely then.

"When I heard the other guy say something about any measures needed, and Kennedy said, and again I quote, 'Any and all measures needed. I want that treasure, even if we have to kill all of them.'

"I could hear the venom in his voice. It was beyond scary. I do not know how I did not see the kind of person he is before I ever dated him.

"Anyway, that was enough to get me to get out of there before he saw me. Since I had already done my presentation, I just eased away from the table, and then headed over to Reggie's place. But he was gone.

"I checked his office this morning and no luck, of course. I decided to go over to your guys' office, since I figured it had something to do with you or someone working for you. The lady in the office told me you had left on a job.

"That is when I headed down to the dock and talked Gilmore into taking me out after you. I do not know exactly what is going on. But the words treasure and killing were enough to scare me and decide to tell Reggie and y'all what I heard."

"Kennedy," Reggie said thoughtfully, his eyes on the wall to one side of Lee's head. "That name is ringing a bell. But I can't quite place it."

His eyes snapped to Lee's. She looked over at Cord. He seemed to be thinking as well.

Suddenly he snapped his fingers. "Mary Montebon!" he said. "Mary Montebon died last year from cervical cancer, I believe. She was on the call list..."

"That voice..." Lee said softly. "The two voices..."

"This Kennedy has her phone. He got the call," Reggie added.

"Call?" Magdalena asked.

Cord quickly answered her question. "A conference call to the various families that are involved." He looked at Lee, and when she nodded, he turned back to Magdalena and continued. "Our ancestors... Of the group involved, were pirates, it seems, just after the turn of the 17th century, going into the 18th century. Early seventeen hundreds.

"It is a long story," Cord told Magdalena. "But the gist of it is their pirate ship, the Irish Rose, sank with a large amount of treasure on board. They got out of the pirate business, got pardons from the Spanish authorities, and settled down.

"They managed to keep their former life secret apparently, and there were never any repercussions. But they, and those with them, were prosperous, and each had children who had children and so forth.

"And we are the current set of descendants. We only found out about the ship having sunk with treasure on it. The call was to let the rest of the families know about it, and see if any wanted to go on the attempt to recover it. Even with getting a share, none seemed at all interested.

"Except one. Right at the end. They had not spoken during the call until right then. I think it was, 'You are so clueless.' or something like that. And a woman's laughter."

Magdalena's eyes snapped up to Cord's. "Sort of deep and low for a woman, but with a sort of hitch at the end?"

The three looked at her before exchanging glances. "Exactly," Cord said, his eyes intense on hers.

"That was Claudia. Kennedy's... Whatever... And Kennedy uses 'clueless' all the time. He thinks everyone is, except himself. He is an arrogant... Well. He is arrogant."

"And dangerous it sounds like," Reggie mused. He looked over at Lee. The others saw his reluctance, but Reggie spoke anyway. "Perhaps we should turn back and drop you and Magdalena off before we head back out to find the ship."

Lee stared at him for a long moment before speaking. "Not on your life, Reggie. I am seeing this thing through." She looked over at Magdalena. "But we can drop Magdalena off or have her picked up by Gilmore."

"I would like to go with you," Magdalena said.

Cord noticed the steel in her voice, and could see some in her backbone, the way she was not sitting tensely.

"That SOB Kennedy... I owe him for what he put me through. I do not want him getting that treasure. And I sure do not want him hurting anyone."

This time Lee made a snap decision. "Okay. You are with us. Cord, show her to a cabin. We are close enough to the same size, I have some clothing you can use. If that is acceptable?"

Magdalena nodded. "Sure. That will be fine. And I can bunk with Reggie if space is tight. We have shared rooms before without any problems."

"We have the room," Lee said immediately. "I am heading back up to the bridge. I think we need to expedite as much as we can."

And then she was up and gone, leaving the others looking at the door she had gone through.

"Um..." Cord said, bringing Magdalena's attention back to him. "I'll show you the cabin." It was more question than statement.

"Sure," Magdalena replied and stood up.

Cord could not keep his eyes off of her as they went down to the next deck where the living quarters were. He introduced her and explained that she was going with them to each of the crew they ran into.

Reluctantly, Cord left her at the cabin to freshen up. He went back up to the bridge. Magdalena would join them shortly.

Once they were all on the bridge again, with Lee at the helm, she upped the throttles slightly, getting to the maximum comfortable speed for the weather and sea conditions. The further they went out the cooler it was, the more wind they encountered, and thus somewhat rougher seas.

Lee kept the crew informed of the conditions as they went about their business so none would be caught off guard.

Cord and Reggie were at one of the secondary navigation displays, showing Magdalena the location where they were as sure as could be the Irish Rose lay in the deep water offshore.

"Cord," Lee said after they looked away from the monitor. She glanced over as the three took the few steps needed to join her.

"Yeah?" Cord asked.

"I'm thinking we might want to give the crew members a chance to opt out of this. It is dangerous enough just diving as often as not. If someone is willing to kill for this treasure... I don't know. I do not want anyone to get hurt."

Cord was nodding. "You're right, Sis. This is personal business. I don't think we have the right to ask our employees to take these kinds of potential risks for something that is not business related.

"I mean sure, we'll give them bonuses and such... But still..."

"I agree," Reggie said as Cord's voice faded away. "And I can get some people to crew under these conditions. They are not highly experienced recovery divers but they are experienced divers. And, to put it bluntly, they are people that can handle themselves. A couple of them owe me, and the others go where those two do."

Lee and Magdalena were both looking at Reggie rather strangely. And then Cord when he said, "You do know some interesting people. Okay. I'll talk to the crew. Give them the option to go back. We can have Gilmore come out and get them. I guess he could bring out Reggie's guys, too. We'd just keep going while that exchange takes place."

"That would work," Lee said. Again, she looked at Reggie. "These guys you know... They... Are they safe?"

Again, her eyes and Magdalena's were on Reggie when he replied. "Well... Safe for us... You all. But not so much to anyone that might want to hurt any of us. These are some salty people."

Lee nodded and turned back to the helm console.

"Okay," Cord said, "I'll go talk to the crew. And Reggie, if you want to check on your guys... See if they are available?"

Reggie smiled slightly. "They'll be available," he said, drawing yet another set of looks from Lee and Magdalena. Who then shared an eyebrow raised glance at his cryptic words and the tone of voice he was using during the discussion.

Magdalena showed an interest in the operation of the ship, so Lee showed her what she could from the helm. "I'm sure Cord will give you a tour later, if you ask him," she said finally.

Lee noticed the sparkle in Magdalena's eyes when she said, "I might just do that."

Considering some of the aggravations she had suffered at Cord's hands over the years, Lee decided to add, "And just FYI. He isn't seeing anyone right now. Hasn't for some time. You know. Just a point of information."

"Well... Okay... Thanks. That is good to know. And thanks for the bridge tour. I think I will go see if I can find Reggie. We need to catch up on some actual family business, too, while we have the chance."

"Okay, Magdalena. I'll be down when I'm relieved at twelve."

"Okay. I will see you then."

Lee was beginning to wonder what Cord and Reggie might be up to since neither one had come back up to the bridge. She had just adjusted the course to head south, now well away from the coast, beyond normal local activity, and even outside or at the very edge of any likely radar scans in the area.

When Lee reached the galley lunch was already prepared, and Cord, Reggie and Magdalena were at the same table they had used before.

As usual, Cord dug in without a word. "Well?" Lee finally asked, when Reggie also began eating.

"Well, what?" asked Cord.

Lee shook her head slightly and rolled her eyes. "The crew, Cord? The crew you were going to talk to? See who wanted to go home?"

Magdalena grinned when Reggie started and winced. Apparently, Lee had kicked him gently under the table. "And you were going to talk to... some people? Why am I sitting here without a single clue about what has happened in the last few minutes?"

"Oh..." Cord said, looking up and over at Lee. When his glance went to Magdalena, he quickly reached for a napkin and wiped his mouth before he spoke again.

"Yeah. About that, Sis." Cord shrugged slightly. "They all want to stay. See it through. You know how they are. Loyal to a fault. And not adverse to a bit of... Excitement."

"Excitement, huh?" Lee asked, frowning. "You did make it clear that excitement could include people with guns and no compunction to not kill someone?"

"Yes, I did, Lee. Think about it."

Rather reluctantly Lee did. And had to admit that she really was not too surprised at the crew members' reactions.

After a few seconds Lee responded "Yes. Okay. You probably did." Lee looked over at Reggie. "At least you won't have to call your people and put them into danger."

Magdalena chuckled when Reggie looked a bit sheepish "Actually, they said they were coming down anyway. I tried to talk them out of it. That I was just checking in with them to see if they would be available, as you said. That I... we... might need their expertise... at some point. They all said they would just go ahead and come down to see what was going on. Kind of a just-in-case thing."

"I see," Lee replied. "They won't be a problem, will they?"

Now Reggie had a slight smile on his face. "Again, not for us. But they would be very bad news to anyone that might need a bit of bad news in their life."

"Oh, great," muttered Lee.

After serving herself and taking a few bites of lunch, Lee looked over at Reggie again. "Reggie, just how do you know these people you are talking about?"

She saw Reggie seem to freeze solid, the fork in his hand midway between plate and his mouth. He was looking across the table, at nothing. It was several moments before he lowered the fork and turned to look at Lee.

"I... Well... It is a bit complicated."

It was Magdalena that spoke, before Lee could, to ask the same question she was about to ask. "Complicated? How can just knowing someone be complicated?"

Cord looked at each one in turn. And decided that Lee could handle things. "Reggie can't really say much about these people," Cord explained. "They are the type of people you know, but don't talk about, because if you do, it could get them killed.

"But they are the type that will lend a hand to anyone that has ever done them an important favor. So, if you two don't mind, it would be a lot easier on Reggie if you dropped it. I know guys like these and they would appreciate it, as well."

"I..." Lee hesitated, wondering just how well she knew Reggie. She thought she knew him very well. But now... "Okay. Yes, of course. Never mind Reggie. But thank you for having them... Available."

Reggie relaxed. A sincere look on his face, he said "Thank you, Lee. That means... Anyway, thanks."

Lee nodded, feeling a bit impressed for reasons she could not explain.

Magdalena was still staring at Reggie. She cut her eyes over to Cord suddenly. "You said you knew guys like the ones Reggie does?"

Cord's cheeks pinked slightly. "Uh... Yeah. I guess..."

"You guess?" She looked at Reggie again. "And you..." She paused, shook her head, then muttered, "Men!"

It drew a chuckle from Lee, as she was feeling much the same.

More relaxed now, the four finished their lunch. Afterwards Lee took Magdalena to get her some clothes to wear. She was very tempted to quiz her about Reggie, but decided it would be far too awkward. She wound up with a bit of information anyway.

Magdalena was holding the small bundle of clothing to her chest, ready to leave Lee's cabin. She paused, the door open, and spoke quietly.

"You know, Lee, Reggie really is a good guy. He has never told me what happened between you two, but I know it tore him up. And seeing how you look at him at times, and he looks at you, there is something there.

"I know we just met, but I can tell you are one of the good ones. Like Reggie. So, I'm telling you, that a bit of risk will be well worth it with Reggie."

With that, she left, to go to the cabin she was using, just down the passage.

Lee stared after her. She heard someone coming and turned around. It was one of the crew, headed toward her with a gear bag. "Hey Lee. Brought a couple of those new suits I've been working on. Thought you and Cord might give them a try on this trip. I don't have one for Reggie. Don't have his measurements."

"Thanks, Gail. You have a real talent with diving gear. That last suit was good. Just needed a few minor changes."

Gail grinned. She hefted the gear bag slightly. "Yep. And they are incorporated into these. Along with a couple of other things I need your opinion on after a bit of use. I know this probably isn't the best trip to do testing, but I wanted to give you the suits now, while we had the chance."

"Of course," Lee replied.

"Thanks, Boss." Gail swung the bag around and handed it to Lee. Lee placed it in her cabin and the two women went back up to the main deck to do some preliminary work for the first dive that would be made upon arrival.

There was not much talking, other than that directly related to what they were doing with the equipment and supplies. There was, however, an undercurrent of tension now that everyone was aware of the possible dangers ahead.

Lee found herself working closely with Reggie without realizing it. Well, until she did realize it and marveled a bit at how comfortable she had been while doing so. Just as they always had in the past.

She as much felt as saw Reggie tense up slightly, and the change in his eyes when she had the realization, and due to it had withdrawn, ever so slightly, from him.

There were no other signs of the sudden discomfort between them, but it was there again, and both knew it.

Twice Lee had to laugh at Cord, when he was in the middle of something and needed a hand and Magdalena was right there and provided that hand.

She had not seen her brother stutter or nearly fall overboard due to a woman since he was thirteen years old. Deciding to not try and tease him at the moment, Lee was sure she would have plenty of chances later. Those two times she just let it slide.

The third was just so good Lee could simply not resist. Keeping from laughing and giving it away, Lee approached the two, their arms up to reach the rigging on one of the hoists.

This had put their bodies face to face but slightly separated. Magdalena was on her tiptoes, both concentrating intensely on getting the locking bolts in place securely.

When Lee called to Cord the two of them started with surprise, causing Magdalena to drop back down off her toes. That caused her to go forward, with even more momentum from her arms swinging down, and put her full up against Cord.

Cord had to grab Magdalena to keep her from falling, which would have knocked him down as well. The two wound up in what amounted to an intimate embrace.

Lee found her eyes widening as neither of the two tried to step back, Cord looking into Magdalena's eyes just as intensely as she was looking into his.

Cord obviously realized what he was doing, and suddenly did step back. Though his hands seemed reluctant to release hers as his slid down her arms, finally taking Magdalena's hands in his.

Lee could not make out what he said to Magdalena, but he was blushing, and she did as well. And the two apparently decided each needed to do something else, as they walked away from the hoist.

Cord also had apparently forgotten that Lee had called to him, for she had to call his name twice more to get his attention. It might not have been a full-on blush, but Cord's face definitely colored slightly when he turned to look at her and realized she had probably seen what had just happened.

Cord did not let on, so Lee did not either. "Cord, Gail brought another set of diving suits for us to try. Do you think we should check them out on this trip? At first I was just going to use them as we have in the past, but with the other risks now..."

Cord thought a moment, and then asked, "These the improved shark resistant and shark repellent suits?"

Lee nodded.

"With where that wreck is, it might be a good idea. I trust her more than enough to use them in these circumstances. And anyway, we might have to go to the hard suits if the wreck wound up deeper than we think."

"Good. That is what I was thinking." Lee stepped a bit closer and lowered her voice. "Is this going to be worth it, Cord?"

"We will drop it as soon as you give the word, Lee," Cord replied, just as quietly. "I do not want anyone hurt. Not you, not Reggie, not the crew..." There was a moment of hesitation when Cord's eyes cut to Magdalena, and then quickly back to Lee's. "Not anyone."

With a nod, Lee headed back into the ship to get the suits and get them ready.

The two days it took them to divert around some bad weather and reach the dive site had them all ready and the ship ready to start working immediately.

Although they had avoided bad weather to get there, bad weather was still affecting the area. And, unfortunately, even more serious weather would hit the area within a few days. That put them in a time crunch that they felt immediately.

Though it was near dark when they took up station, Cord and Lee suited up and went down, just to check the conditions. Reggie and Magdalena were watching the monitors for the cameras that were integrated into Cord's and Lee's dive equipment.

They did not stay down long. After they stripped off the dive gear, dressed, and had cups of hot chocolate in their hands, they and Reggie and Magdalena gathered around the chart table while the crew was getting the ship ready for staying overnight on station.

"The water is clear at the moment," Cord said after his first sip of hot chocolate. "We went down far enough to be able to see the slope from shore."

"It was steep," Lee added when Cord took another sip of the hot chocolate. "It is almost certain the Irish Rose is down deep. Our initial look confirms the charts right here. That suggests that we can be fairly certain they are accurate in the rest of the area."

"Yes," Cord said. "Which means," he added, "that if we have interpreted everything from the journals correctly, the Irish Rose is at the base of this slope somewhere. Exactly where is the question."

"And whether or not she is broken up or buried from run-off from land." Reggie was looking thoughtful.

"Or has been carried out further." Lee also looked thoughtful. "Though..."

"Yes," Magdalena said, "There are still unknowns..."

With that comment, the four headed down to eat before turning in for the night, with the expectation of getting an early start the next day.

And they were up and ready early. And though the seas were calm, the clouds were low and heavy, with light rains coming down steadily.

That did not slow down the operation, however. Cord, Lee, and Reggie were all ready for a long dive when the crew had the support gear ready.

When the three entered the water from the dive compartment in the lowest deck of the ship, each had a scooter equipped with high intensity lights, extra dive gasses, and enough battery power for an extended run with the powerful drives.

By the end of the day, with twilight coming early, they had explored the area below them thoroughly, having made it all the way to the bottom in that area.

They had relocated the Camille twice, and had enough time to get ready for the first dive the next morning before settling in for the night.

There were long swells coming in toward shore the next morning, with the steady rain more intense, and occasional thunderstorms with lightning.

It was risky, but Cord, Lee, and Reggie all agreed that the risk was worth it, and began the first dive as soon as things could be made ready.

Magdalena jumped slightly when Lee let out a shout. Or as much of a shout as was possible in the dive mask. Magdalena fiddled with the camera and monitor controls, trying to get a better look at what Lee had obviously seen.

With the stronger wave action, and the somewhat shallower depth of the water at that point, there was more sediment being stirred up than the other areas they had checked.

As Lee dove deeper, getting closer to whatever it was, and then Cord and Reggie joined her, adding the light from their scooters and headlamps to that of Lee's, Magdalena finally got a good look at what the three divers were seeing.

There was no mistaking it. It was the Irish Rose. And Magdalena thought it looked to be in remarkably good shape. Though Lee, Cord, and Reggie would be able to tell much better.

Their air time was running low, so a buoy was anchored and deployed. It would float up to just under the surface of the water. If a signal was received, the buoy would respond so it could be located.

The ship was not having any trouble maintaining station, but all thought it prudent to have the backup of the locator buoy in place. Magdalena was waiting for them in the chart room when they were ready to take a break before going back down.

It was an excited trio that came in and sat down. "I can't believe it!" Lee exclaimed. "It looks like she simply settled down vertically. I am not sure she even touched the slope on the way down."

"I have to agree," Reggie, his eyes glowing as he looked at Lee.

"Yep," Cord added. "From what was described in the journal, the Irish Rose ran aground hard, and stove in the hull in two places. But with as strongly as she was built, Markus had noted in the log that he thought that they would be able to make repairs after the hurricane was over. They did not get the chance, of course, as it floated free with the incoming tide and storm surge.

"Which, of course, with the wave action, then pulled the Irish Rose off the barrier and out far enough for her to sink."

"The ballast and general design kept her upright, though, from the looks of things," Reggie said. "She was... Is... An excellent design and was well built. With the water she had taken on between the time of the impact to when she was freed, she did go down pretty quickly, I would think."

"Why is she so far out, though?" Magdalena asked. "Especially if she went down fast, why didn't she go down the slope?"

The other three looked at one another. Cord shrugged. Lee shook her head. Only Reggie offered a theory. "I think it might have been a combination of a wind change, which is noted in the log, and a couple of comments in two of the journals.

"Plus, though there is no way to know for sure, it is possible... Probable... That it was more storm surge than tide that lifted the Irish Rose. And the hurricane was still moving pretty fast at the time, so if the tide was going out, the storm surge was lessening, and the winds had changed, I think the Irish Rose just sailed away from the barrier as she sank.

"At least far enough to clear the slope of the land. And since she was somewhat heavy aft with the water accumulation, she would have had a bit of aft way even as she went down, until fully filled with water."

Lee and Cord exchanged a look. "She is sitting with her bow toward the coast," Lee said.

"And she is down deeper in the mud aft," Cord said musingly.

"So, Reggie could be right?" Magdalena asked.

Without thinking, Lee reached over and squeezed his hand as she smiled and said, "He is... Always has been a very logical thinker. It is one of the things I..." She gasped, without finishing her thought, which annoyed Reggie no end and Cord found funny. Until it became obvious that the jolt and the noise that had caused Lee to stop talking was of more importance than what Lee was saying.

All four scrambled up from their seats, but before any of them could do anything, there were five more people in the chart room, all with guns of one kind or another in their hands. All pointed at the four.

"What..." was all that Cord got out before the obvious leader of the group cut him off.

"Shut up." He was not looking at Cord. He was looking at Magdalena. "Well, well, well... Claudia was right..."

The woman in the group, also well-armed and looking like she was both able and willing to use her weapon, almost eager actually, said, "I told you so, Kennedy. I told you that was her leaving."

"Shut up, Claudia."

Kennedy had not taken his eyes off Magdalena. A quick step forward, and before anyone could do a thing, he backhanded Magdalena across the face. She staggered back with a cry, almost falling. Lee was able to catch her before she went down.

Cord beat Reggie in getting between Magdalena and Kennedy. Cord was going for Kennedy with rage in his eyes, but four guns were suddenly in his face. He stopped, glaring at Kennedy, who had a slight smile on his face. He looked over at Magdalena, now standing straight, the left side of her face bright red, her left eye already beginning to swell shut.

"Never should have walked out on me, Mags. Nobody walks on me unless I tell them to leave. And now here you are. What a coincidence you saw me at that thing, and now here you are with my ex-in-laws. Who are about to come into some significant money."

Cord had managed to calm down slightly, with Reggie's hand on his arm, partly to be able to restrain him if needed, but also to show that he was there with him.

"My crew?" Cord asked tightly.

Kennedy moved back, as did the others, their guns still trained on the four. "Fine. For the moment. Few bruises, I must admit," Kennedy said with a chuckle. "Some feisty women on this boat."

Reggie's hand on his arm kept Cord from moving, but Magdalena had to grab Lee when she started for Kennedy. "If you hurt any…"

This time Reggie and Cord got between Kennedy and Lee before Kennedy could step forward and strike her. "Easy," Cord told Lee softly.

"Oh, it will not be me that hurts them," Kennedy said with a laugh. "Claudia here is the one that likes to inflict pain. Especially on other women."

"What do you want?" asked Reggie. Lee noted his calm voice, but could see the restrained energy in his body.

"What do I want?" bellowed Kennedy. He took a step toward Reggie, but something made him stop before getting within reaching range. "I want the treasure, you idiot! What else would I want? Do some fishing? I. Want. That. Treasure!"

"You're welcome to go down and get it," Cord said, also now under tight control.

"Oh," Kennedy said, "I think I will stay up here, nice and warm and dry." His voice hardened. "You four, however, along with two of my men, will go down, do what it is you do and bring my treasure up to me."

"Magdalena can't…" Reggie was saying, intending to tell Kennedy that she could not dive. She did not have the experience for this, and with the swelling in her face, especially around the eye, it would be too dangerous.

"It's okay, Reggie," Magdalena said.

When Reggie turned his head to look at her and protest, he could see the pleading in her eyes, and so could Cord. She did not want to be up here with Kennedy, and especially Claudia.

Reggie nodded.

"Well," laughed Kennedy, "that seems to be settled, fortunately for all of your sakes. And the crews. No need to waste any more time. Get on it." And when he added the, "NOW," there was no question that he would not back down.

Reggie, Magdalena, Lee, and Cord did not even bother to protest. They were watched closely as they moved from the chart room down into the work area to get ready to dive.

The fact that it was already dark made no difference. It would be dark in the water in the daytime anyway, and the work areas on board were well lighted.

Magdalena heard Lee growl slightly when they saw the already forming bruises on Gail's face and arms, as well as those on a couple of the men, one of whom was limping, when the dive support crew entered. They had obviously put up a struggle.

With only soft exchanges about equipment and the dive, the four suited up. Two of Kennedy's men were already in suits, with tanks on their backs. And wicked spear guns in their hands.

When Reggie, Magdalena, Cord, and Lee started to strap on the dive knives Kennedy spoke up. "Don't think so, people. No knives for you."

"But…" Lee started to protest.

A hard look from Kennedy and an eager one from Claudia had the protest dying on Lee's lips. She turned away and the four began checking each other's gear as the final step before entering the water.

Kennedy motioned for one of his men to drop through the dive hatch first. Reggie, Cord, Magdalena, and Lee followed, with Kennedy's second diver joining them last.

Kennedy and Claudia hurried over to the monitors the dive crew were watching. There was silence for a long time as those in the water went down, deeper and deeper. Suddenly, one of Kennedy's men stopped. When Cord turned his head to look at him, the camera on his dive helmet caught the panicked look on the man's face.

They watched as the man suddenly shifted position and then began to swim straight up. Far too fast to be safe.

"What's going on, Roberts?" shouted Kennedy into the console microphone.

The only reply was whimpering and gasping for breath. Roberts was rising faster than his air bubbles. He was still going when he got beyond the range of the cameras.

"We'll go see about…" Cord began saying, as he shifted position to swim up, rather than down.

"No," Kennedy commanded. "Keep going. I want that treasure!"

Without another word the dive continued. It was only a few more minutes before they reached the Irish Rose in her watery grave. "I want to see the treasure! Go in and show me the treasure!" Kennedy shouted into the mic.

"It's too dangerous," Lee replied as the group held position a few feet from the ship. "We need to…"

"Now!" screamed Kennedy. "Make them go in, Masters. Shoot one of them. The rest will go."

Masters seemed ready to do as ordered, but he did not need to as Cord, Lee, Reggie and Magdalena swam toward the ship and then toward the uncovered cargo hatch.

Lee saw the object first. She swam a bit closer to the silt covered lump on the deck by the hatch. A swirl of water created by a hand motion had the sediment rising and drifting away. The shine of bright gold was almost glaring in the lights the divers wore and carried.

"Bring it up! Bring it up! Now! I want to see it. Hold it in my hands!" Kennedy shouted.

Even Claudia gave him a strange look at his ranting.

Lee picked up the object, but Masters was right there and took it from her. He headed up quickly, but just as quickly slowed his ascent when he started to rise faster than his bubbles.

Maintaining a safer rate of ascent, the others went up even slower, not willing to take any chances. Masters was already aboard the ship when the other four approached from below.

It took a moment for them to figure out why the water was a bit cloudy. When they saw the body of Roberts bumping against the hull of the ship, his mask gone and blood seeping from his eyes, nose, and mouth, it was pretty obvious. Blood in the water.

The four were suddenly exchanging worried glances. And then they were all scanning the water in a different direction as they swam slowly toward the dive hatch in the hull of the ship.

They still had several feet to go before the first shark showed up. It was a small one, but they all recognized it as a bull shark. Bull sharks were aggressive and where the breed of shark most likely to attack humans. And were the breed that made the majority of the human shark attacks in American waters.

Despite trying to prevent them, Cord and Reggie moved between Lee and Magdalena as they continued to swim slowly toward the hatch. The shark found Roberts' body and began to feed.

Seconds later two more bull sharks showed up, both larger than the first, and joined in the feast.

Cord and Reggie got Lee and Magdalena up through the dive hatch and then joined them in the dive compartment. As they removed their dive helmets, they saw Masters slumped partly on and partly off a small sit-down bench. He was pale and his breathing was raspy. Cord and Reggie exchanged a look. Masters, though he had slowed, had still risen too fast for safety. Without being put into the decompression chamber he was a goner.

Lee looked over and realized the same thing. She joined Cord and Reggie, with Magdalena on her heels. "Decompression…" Lee said, but a shake of Cord's head silenced her. She frowned, but with a look at Kennedy and Claudia, and then the spear gun on the deck by Masters, she decided the man had chosen his path.

"Let me see!" Claudia said loudly, drawing looks from the four.

They saw Kennedy push Claudia away. "NO! It's mine!"

Kennedy was holding the large, gem encrusted, gold cross reverently. And not because of its religious aspects.

Kennedy's other man was looking around, rather worriedly. Claudia and Kennedy were engrossed in the artifact. Roberts had not returned, and Masters was obviously out of it.

He was now keeping his gun on Cord, Lee, Reggie and Magdalena. The dive crew, grouped together at the end of the console, were in the peripheral vision of the man. They had caused no trouble during the dive, and he decided they were tamed. It was the divers he was worried about.

The man was wrong, about several things, the most important being the dive crew being tamed. Cord and Lee were watching the crew. A few hand signals from them, and Cord and Lee both nodded.

"Get ready," Lee whispered to Reggie and Magdalena.

Suddenly the dive crew began to move. Very, very quickly. One moved toward the guard, pulling a wrench up from behind his leg where he had been hiding it. The other three, including Gail, tackled Claudia and Kennedy.

They had no intention of trying to overpower them. Cord had insisted that they just get them off balance and down, their weapons out of reach. They were successful. With the guard now down, groaning, a major lump forming on the shoulder of his gun arm, his submachine gun across the room from him, Cord, Lee and the rest ran for the hatchways.

Cord, Lee, Reggie and Magdalena took one corridor, toward the bow, while the dive crew headed aft and up toward the rear deck.

Even with several bulkheads between them, the open hatches allowed the bellowed scream of Kennedy to be heard by everyone on the ship. He was still screaming obscenities as he picked up his gun and ran toward the hatch he had seen Magdalena go through. Claudia was not far behind, though she was silent.

Cord headed for the arms locker on the bridge when he got there. Magdalena and Reggie were watching the hatches and out the ports, while Lee was using the internal cameras to watch the passageways and decks.

The three men guarding the rest of the crew who were locked away in one of the crew compartments, though obviously nervous, stayed where they were. Lee sighed in relief when Gail and the rest of the dive crew made it to the aft deck and took cover behind some of the machinery. Without night vision they would be almost impossible to find by one or two people doing a search, even with flashlights.

"He's two decks below us," Lee suddenly said. The other three did not need to ask who 'he' was. "Passing through the kitchen and dining area."

Cord began passing out the weapons kept in the arms locker. Armed himself, he began to take a look at the radios that had been smashed by Kennedy's men. He had hoped to possibly get one of them working, but that was not going to happen.

Having been keeping track of Kennedy, Lee missed the other guard, now recovered though with an aching shoulder as he approached the port side hatch of the bridge. He wanted some revenge for being humiliated in the dive compartment.

"He's coming through!" Lee called, and spun around, her handgun up, facing the hatch that Kennedy and Claudia would come through in just moments.

Their attention elsewhere, the guard decided it was as good a time as any. He eased the hatch open and stepped inside quietly. Even though the weather had worsened, with rain now falling steadily and the swells changing to chop, it was several long moments before Lee started to turn to look where the cold air and sounds were coming from, but the guard was already on her, his arm around her waist, the gun in his hand coming down on her hand holding her handgun, knocking it free. When he lifted his gun to her temple and the other three on the bridge were turning to look, Kennedy burst through the hatch, Claudia entering right behind him.

Kennedy and Claudia were both breathing heavily, but for different reasons. Kennedy was enraged. Claudia was winded, but the result was the same. Their hands were shaking, making holding their guns steady impossible.

The guard held all the cards, however, with a gun to Lee's temple. He was a big man, and without him giving her an opening, Lee would not be able to break away without getting a bullet in her head.

"Okay," Kennedy bellowed. "Drop 'em! He'll blow her brains out!" Kennedy did not know how it had happened, and did not care, but he would take advantage of what his man had accomplished.

Reluctantly, Cord, Reggie and Magdalena squatted down and put their handguns on the deck.

"Out!" Kennedy shouted, his voice down from the bellow at least slightly. "You are going back down. Right now. I want more of the treasure tonight!"

"We can't…" Cord protested. He stopped when the guard squeezed Lee's waist more tightly and pressed the muzzle of his gun harder into her temple, causing her to let a groan escape.

"Sharks, Kennedy," Magdalena pleaded. "The other diver… blood in the water… there are sharks everywhere now."

"Well, isn't that a development? Too bad, Mags. You are all going down again. I want more and I want it now!" His voice had risen during his tirade, ending with it nearly being a scream.

The guard began to move with Lee toward the hatch behind Kennedy and Claudia. When Kennedy motioned with his gun, Cord, Lee and Reggie moved that way as well.

The rain was pouring now, with gusty winds blowing spray off the tops of the growing waves. When the guard started to take Lee through the hatch that led to the kitchen and dining area Kennedy spoke again, this time in a normal tone of voice.

"No. Crew could be anywhere. Down on the open deck. We'll go down from there."

The guard finally had to turn loose of Lee to be able to get down the stairs leading down from deck to deck. It was when they were all standing near the starboard rail of the rear deck, not too far from where the compartments were when things suddenly happened without warning.

Four men, in black wet suits, holding black weapons, rose up from the deck only a few feet from the group. "Everyone put down your weapons. Quickly now!" came a commanding voice.

They could all hear the very slight sound coming from the earpieces in the left ear of each of the four men. The one that had told them to put down their weapons spoke quietly, obviously using a radio. "Roger. Secure the tangos and release the crew but keep them there."

"Who are you?" Kennedy said, again nearly screaming. Though the guard and Claudia had both put down their guns, Kennedy still held onto his tightly, even with shaking hands.

"A friend of a friend. Now put down the gun or I will shoot you."

"You can't have the treasure! That treasure is mine!" screamed Kennedy.

"Is he always this crazy?" asked the wet suited man. No answer came, but when Kennedy moved the gun again, there was a pfft sound and Kennedy went down on the deck silently. "Tranq," said the man, holstering the handgun. He turned to his men, who still had guns trained on Claudia and the guard. "Signal the Coast Guard," he told one of them.

The man raised a radio in a water proof bag and spoke a few words that the rest could not hear.

When the sound of a Coast Guard vessel warning siren cut through the sounds of the growing storm Claudia looked around. Kennedy was down. They would all be going to jail.

Turning wild eyes to Magdalena, Claudia lunged. She was quick and no one was expecting the crazy move. When Claudia's body slammed into Magdalena, Magdalena rammed into Lee, and the two women went over the rail into the water without a sound.

Claudia and the guard were quickly taken down and secured on the deck. Claudia was now crying and wailing, with the occasional statement that it was all Kennedy's idea and he made her do it. She kept thrashing around until one of the rescue team literally sat on her.

The deck lights came on, and the lights of the Coast Guard cutter continued to approach, though thankfully the siren was cut off.

While that was all occurring, both Reggie and Cord had dived over the rail a mere fraction of a second after Lee and Magdalena had gone over. Wild confusion reigned for many long moments, but Reggie shouted up that he had Lee, and then almost immediately Cord added his, "I have Magdalena! I think she's hurt. Get us up!"

CHAPTER EIGHT

Eighteen months later…

It had taken that long to get everything ready for this particular day. A month of dealing with the authorities over the attack and seeing that justice was done for Kennedy, Claudia, and the other surviving members of that criminal enterprise.

It turned out the attack on board the Camille was only a side issue with Kennedy. Everything came out during the investigation about his other criminal activities.

Another month passed before Lee and Magdalena were both up to going back out to the location, which both insisted upon. Cord did make good use of the time, making further arrangements for recovering everything possible from the Irish Rose. Not only that, but to also raise the ship itself after having seen how well she was preserved.

Those two months for Cord were not just spent with the authorities or getting the additional preparations readied on the Camille. Cord spent quite a bit of the time getting to know Magdalena better. And she was happily providing the information, and learning about Cord as well.

It did not take much for Lee to totally forgive Reggie, and even admit she had possibly overreacted a bit. Reggie wasted no time furthering his cause with her.

The other occasional delays were all work related, for Reggie and Lee and Cord. Magdalena, who needed more recovery time due to her injuries, had given her notice to her employer shortly after their return to shore, so had plenty of time to recover then do much of the planning and design work on the plans the four of them had agreed upon after dealing with the IRS and the state income tax people.

Due to the skills and experience that Lee and Cord had, as well as the quality equipment and detail planning always present in their work, the raising of the Irish Rose was a relatively simple job.

Then came the day to use the float bags to raise the Irish Rose. Those on the Camille along with two other support ships, and Reggie's Seal Team buddies all let out an amazed gasp when the Irish Rose's still intact masts first broke the surface of the water. When the upper part of the ship itself came into view, there came a rousing cheer.

After they secured her, still mostly submerged, the Irish Rose was towed to where she would be pulled from the water so the restoration work could begin. The process of restoring her, recreating the missing long boats, and the few other items that were not recovered took the rest of the eighteen months.

Many other things were taking place, as well, but everything was ready for what Magdalena had begun calling, "The Day."

"Thank the Lord this is almost over," Cord said, looking around the edge of the screen set up to conceal from the crowd anything and everything that was occurring behind it and the several others that lined the pier.

There were even screens that went out into the water and hid something that was in the water next to the pier. Large drapes hid what was obviously signage on the new building on shore at the land end of the pier.

Lee slapped his arm. "Cord! That is not something you say on your wedding day!"

Cord turned startled eyes onto his sister. "I didn't mean…" he nearly stuttered, panic in his eyes.

"Calm down, calm down," Lee soothed, even though she was grinning. "I was just kidding. I knew what you meant. The exhibit…"

"Yes," Cord replied, looking toward the screens hiding whatever it was in the water.

When Cord stepped back, away from the screen, Lee reached out and touched his arm. When he turned toward her, she reached up to fiddle with the bow tie of his tuxedo. It really did not need any adjustment, but she needed something to do with her hands.

After a few moments of just holding her hands against Cord's shoulders she lifted her head and met his eyes.

"I love you, Sis," Cord said softly.

"And I you," Lee said in return. "I can't believe we are both getting married, and on the same day." The words were almost breathless.

Cord looked over at yet another screen and added quietly. "I know. I never really thought I would ever marry. But Magdalena… She's… She…"

Lee had to chuckle. "Are you trying to say, dear brother, that… I think the saying goes… 'She's all that. And more.'?"

"Well… yeah," Cord said, rather sheepishly. Then he grinned. "And I have to tell you, I knew all along that you would finally realize just how much Reggie loves you, and that he had not done what you thought he had, and you would forgive him for not making it clear much sooner.

"Oh. And how much you love him. And always have."

Suddenly a distant look formed in Lee's eyes. "Yes," she said, almost dreamily Cord decided, "I do love him. Even when I was hating him, I loved him."

The two turned before the conversation could continue when Cord's best man, Dudley Hudson, came toward them. "Everyone is ready, if you two are," he said, his northeastern accent very obvious here in the south.

Cord and Lee exchanged looks and then both turned back to Dudley and nodded. Dudley smiled. "I shall start the proceedings then."

Cord was about to ask Lee to loosen the death grip she had on his arm as they got ready to walk down the aisle, but suddenly no longer noticed it. The music had started.

When they stepped around the screen both sets of eyes went toward the other end of the aisle that had been created. Reggie, with Magdalena on his arm, was approaching the center of the aisle where the priest, Dudley, Lee and Magdalena's Maid of Honor waited. The two couples could not take their eyes off each other.

Things became something of a blur to the four primary participants. The two brides were given from brother to brother, and the ceremony continued.

Dudley, best man for both of the men, having met and become friends at Harvard Business School with them before Reggie went on to law school, handed out the correct rings to the correct people when asked.

Interesting enough, both Lee and Magdalena had asked the same woman to be her Maid of Honor. Having met at different times, but forming similar bonds, Alexis Beaucheau had been more than a bit startled when she saw who was going to escort her to where the priest waited.

"Dudley! How… What…"

"Alexis! This is quite a surprise. A very nice one, if I might add."

"But…" Alexis knew this was not the time nor place. She quietly took Dudley's arm and then took her place when they reached the priest. Then the two brides and grooms were approaching.

The ceremony over, the two newly married couples walked together, followed by Alexis and Dudley, toward a podium in front of the new building. When they arrived and turned around, they saw the sea of faces of the people that had followed them, along with dozens more, including a large contingent of print, radio and video media people.

Cord stepped to the mic on the podium lectern, with the other three right there beside him. "Ladies and Gentlemen, welcome to our wedding reception. And, I must admit, to something a bit more. This is the grand opening of a new sea faring exhibit that is three hundred years in the making."

Cord stepped back and Lee stepped up. "That is correct, ladies and gentlemen. Three hundred years in the making. And I can tell you that it is a wonderous tale. But I need not tell you myself. The exhibits inside will have all that information, with some pretty impressive graphics, to boot.

"But there is a personal note to this exhibit, as well. Three of us just happen to be the descendants of the people involved three hundred years ago that began this tale."

When Lee stepped back, Reggie stepped up. "Yes. Cord Lynch; his sister Lee, my new wife and I are all distant relatives to Markus and Aislinn Lynch, a brother and sister that came from Ireland in the late seventeenth century to make a new life for themselves."

It was Magdalena's turn. "While I am not an original descendant of the group of people that Markus and Aislinn gathered about them to carve out a successful farm, ranch, and timber operation in what became the State of Georgia, I am proud to say that I am now part of the family."

Cord reached over and squeezed her hand before she continued. "While it is said that almost every family in America that comes from the early settlers probably has a horse thief in their family history, that is not the case with the Lynches. Definitely not."

Magdalena paused, rather dramatically. "No, that is far too mundane for a family like the Lynches. You will see the story inside, but I can tell you now that their skeleton in their historical closet, is not one, but two pirates."

The crowd let out a huge collective gasp. Behind them, sitting quiet to one side, Alexis and Dudley exchanged wide-eyed looks as Magdalena continued.

"Yes, ladies and gentlemen, this museum, and the screened item out by the pier, are dedicated to those ancestors and the pirate ship they sailed upon. The recently found, recovered and restored… Irish Rose!"

Everyone in the audience turned to look. The screens were dropped and there was the Irish Rose, in all her glory, freshly restored to her original condition.

"Now, ladies and gentlemen, please join us in the museum for our wedding reception and the grand opening tour of the museum."

Dudley quickly led the two couples and Alexis out of the way and into the private area of the museum so they could change clothes, whereupon they would go out and mingle with the guests.

Dudley was vastly disappointed when Alexis said she had to leave to catch her flight. She did allow him a quick hug and kiss on the cheek, but that was it. It was not long before he had to leave as well. He could not afford to miss his upcoming meeting. If it went well, he would finally be able to say, even to himself, that he was now successful. Successful in the way that Alexis' father was successful, and in the way that her father expected the man that Alexis would marry would be successful.

Taking a moment to thank Dudley and see him off, the two couples were happy to talk to those there for the wedding as well as those there for the long-awaited mystery museum. Finally, the last guest left. The caterers and cleanup crews left and security was quietly in the background.

Lee sat down on a sofa in the main office of the museum with a sigh. "Wow. That was quite the turn out."

Reggie, taking the seat next to her took her left hand in both of his. "Yes, it was." A kiss on her knuckles and he let his left hand slide from hers and intertwined the fingers of his right hand with those of her left, which was a now familiar and comfortable occurrence.

"I do not know how you did it, Reggie," Cord said, seating Magdalena and then taking a seat himself in the luxurious leather chairs that matched the sofa. Their hands found each other, as well. "I thought several of the families would be here, claiming a share."

Reggie smiled. "Oh, it was not too difficult. With the recording of the phone conversation, and the documents that I sent out for each of them to sign... you know... so they would be 'protected' from the Lynches trying to get money out of them to pay for the fiasco the search would be."

Magdalena laughed. "Pure Reggie," she said.

Reggie smiled. "I was contacted by a couple of attorneys questioning the validity of the agreements. Obviously on behalf of some of the families. Once they understood the full efforts that had been taken to 'protect' the families' good names and their pocketbooks, with their full support, they realized that it was pretty ironclad. The families had been hoist with their own petard.

"Any type of suit against us would bring the entire story out and their names would be forever linked with pirates."

Lee grimaced. "I just do not see the stigma," she said. "But there are people here in the south that set great store in their family histories being as pure as the driven snow.

"There have not been any major repercussions for us admitting... even advertising the fact that we, the Lynches, had ancestors that were pirates. The media was eating it up. Even the people from all three state Historical Societies."

"If anything," Magdalena added, "It has brought some pretty positive notoriety." She laughed. "Especially among the treasure hunting hobbyists and fanatics."

"Exactly," Cord said, then chuckled. "And actually confronting the government and winning the suit that made everything ours, rather than theirs, has given a few people some satisfaction. Those treasure laws are not too well liked."

Reggie nodded. "I was pretty sure there would not be too much trouble. With the provenance we had, all that documentation and the artifacts that have been in our family for all these years, there was no real question as to the fact that our ancestors owned it.

"The proof was there that no charges were ever brought against them, and both the English and Spanish governments had said that the family was entitled to the spoils due to the criminal actions they had endured by Spanish soldiers. Everything clearly belonged to the Lynch family."

"I do think your idea of setting up a trust fund that the other families could access for certain things without any links to us, may have helped," Cord said. He arched his back and stretched.

"That was more Lee, than me," Reggie replied. "When Aunt Maggie would not take anything directly…"

Lee laughed. "Boy, oh boy. She can be a handful. I tried everything I could think of to get her to take some of the money. I offered to buy her a new place. She didn't want one.

"I offered to have the one she owns totally remodeled. No way. New vehicle, a cruise, a trip to Ireland… She would not accept any of it. She said she told us she wouldn't when we were on the phone. And she was sticking to it."

A bit sadly Lee paused, but picked up the story again. "She said she doesn't have much longer. She just wished she had been able to provide for a few people, and a couple of charities, before she dies."

"And that one rather longing statement was enough for Lee to bring to me," Reggie said, squeezing her hand. "I must say she was a bit reluctant to sign off on the trust fund, but finally, I guess, she decided that since she wasn't actually taking any of the money herself, that it would be okay. She did, finally, accept one of the gold coins."

"She was almost bouncing up and down on her scooter today," Lee said and laughed. "She had to see everything in here and on the Irish Rose. The guys helping with the tour were so nice to get her down below decks and back up. And she loved the attention."

Cord smiled, too. "Oh, yes. And when we told her just how much we actually recovered, she was ecstatic."

"Well," Magdalena said with a grin, "I think that was more over us not making it public than what-all we recovered. And that the other families had no idea."

"Good point, Mags," Lee said. "She wasn't too happy we just offered up to pay the taxes on the full amount, but was somewhat mollified when I told her that both the state and the feds worked a deal with us."

"We were going to build the museum, anyway," Cord said.

"And open the Irish Rose to tourists," Magdalena said.

"Well, for whatever the reasons were, and how it worked out, I think we came out like pirates, ourselves," Lee said with a chuckle.

"Shush," Reggie whispered to her.

The others laughed. "Okay, okay. We aren't pirates. But converting everything, through different agencies and brokers, put all those period monetary items, the artifacts, the gems and jewelry, and everything else with historical value in the hands of people that would take good care of them and have them on public view. I mean, look at how much we have on display here." Lee gestured with her free hand, indicating the museum.

"Very true, sister dear," Cord said. "But I like having modern, US minted gold and silver coins in our various stashes and caches. And money in the bank, and converted to our… other assets…"

"Ah," said Reggie, "we were able to get some very good deals on some things."

"We did," Lee said, giving Reggie a firm look. "With the help of your 'friends', the Seals. Are you ever going to tell me how you got involved with them? And why they are so eager to help you?"

Reggie's eyes cut to Cord. Unfortunately, both Lee and Magdalena saw the rather furtive glance.

"Wait a minute!" Magdalena turned to look at Cord, giving him a long look. Lee was doing much the same.

Magdalena then looked over at Lee. "Did it seem like they knew Cord, too?"

"Well… now that you mention it, they did seem to be pretty buddy, buddy, considering they had just met. Or so I thought at the time." Lee glared at Cord. "Or had they?"

"Well," Reggie said quietly, "let's just say that when a person can do something for their country, and it helps good people, then one does it. Even if they can never talk about it."

Reggie's eyes gazed into Lee's for long moments, and then Magdalena's. Cord did the same.

A bit subdued, both women finally nodded. "Okay," Lee finally said. "No more questions about it. But whatever it was… Thank you for doing it. Because it was apparently a very big… thing…"

"Yeah. Me, too," Magdalena said softly. "You guys are way deeper than I ever imagined. And I thought you were both pretty deep as it was."

"Yes. Even raising the Irish Rose you both were more concerned with keeping everyone safe and preserving everything. It was not about the treasure. It was the history." Lee glanced between the two men. She had to smile at the almost embarrassed looks on their faces.

"You're right," agreed Magdalena. She, too, glanced at the two and saw the same slightly reddened faces.

"Okay," Reggie said after a moment. "The security is set, and I, for one, am ready to finish out this day with the first part of our honeymoon trip."

Now it was Lee and Magdalena with red faces. Neither said anything as they rose, with Reggie and Cord getting up as well to lend a hand.

As they headed for the back door of the museum to start their respective honeymoons, Magdalena suddenly asked, "Oh. Someone asked me today why the Irish Rose was so well preserved. He said he was amazed at the condition of the bronze cannon. I am not quite sure about the whys of that, myself."

"Yes," added Lee. "And I am still not clear on just exactly how Kennedy and his crew got on the Camille. Or your friends, either. Care to enlighten us on that, too?

"Ah." Reggie looked over at Cord. "Why don't you explain about the condition of the Irish Rose. She's your wife. I can explain about the RIBs.

Looking at his wife, Reggie said, "Kennedy stole… Or had someone steal a large Rigid Inflatable Boat from a dealership up north. I am kind of surprised a guy like Kennedy was willing to come out as far as we were in one of them, actually.

"Anyway, the thing is really fast and with everything the way it was, no one saw them before they were almost to the Camille. The radar alarm simply did not pick them up due to sea conditions. By the time of the guys hailed them they were at the ship and came aboard with guns pointed. Our guys did not have a chance of stopping them. Though you know they did try."

The others nodded. Reggie continued. "Now, our friends being who they are, new a guy…"

Magdalena and Lee both rolled their eyes.

"Uh-hum… Anyway, as I was saying," Reggie continued, "They new a guy with a helicopter they could borrow. Big enough to bring out two smaller RIBs. Black. Since one of the guys knows the local Coast Guard commander…"

"Of course," Lee said.

"Yes, well… He contacted him and asked him to be on alert. So, she was. Also knowing these guys, she sent a cutter out that way, just on the off chance something happened.

"The gang did not have anyone on lookout, thinking no one would have any clue anything was wrong since they got the drop on us. So, after being dropped off by the helicopter out of visual range of the Camille, our guys came in at high speed and boarded us just before everything happened on deck."

"Well, that explains that," Morgana said. She looked over at Cord.

Cord grinned. "Sure. About why the Irish Rose was so well preserved. Well, you know how the Irish Rose went down, staying upright and gliding downward to make a rather gentle landing on the sea floor, leaving almost everything intact.

"That was during a lull in the hurricane apparently. But the waters were churned up quite a bit from all the wave action, and the river there was dumping huge amounts of silt and debris into the cove and ultimately out further into the ocean.

"You saw the ship on the bottom. It was not buried, but it did have a very thick coating of silt on it. And it got some of that immediately after it went down.

"That silt did not have much of anything highly corrosive or anything that would do significant damage to any of the various parts of the ship in it. At least not that initial coating.

"And it was just deep enough to be cold enough, as you well know having been down there, to help in preserving some of the items that would not have fared well in warmer waters.

"Those oak timbers and planking, and even the masts, were massive to start with, and since much of it was kept well treated against the elements while in use, those same treatments helped the preservation, too.

"All those factors, especially the extraordinary construction and quality of the fittings, cannon, and so many of the other items, all combined to make it possible. I guess that is just simply another element in the tale of the Irish Rose."

None of them could even dream of the further tales that the Irish Rose would one day have to tell.

THE END

MEET THE AUTHOR

Author Jerry D. Young has been a fixture in the survival and prepping communities for more than twenty years. The author of more than 100 novels and short stories, Jerry's writing has been a staple for men and women of all ages and from all walks of life that are interested in prepping, survival, and all-around self-sufficiency. Jerry's books are written with the goal of educating as well as entertaining and generally enjoyed by all who seek to expand their knowledge of prepping and survival topics while enjoying a good book or short story. As daunting as the end of the world, nuclear fallout, World War III, Civil unrest, economic collapse, solar flares, EMP attacks, and other apocalyptic scenarios may be, society has always been interested in the "What If?" of a Post-Apocalyptic World. Jerry's stories provide interesting and practical perspectives of heroes and villains navigating Post-Apocalyptic scenarios including everything from Mad Max type of events to more relevant plot lines that seem as if they could have come from the headlines of the modern world. Find more about Jerry D. Young at www.CreativeTexts.com

THANK YOU FOR READING!

If you enjoyed this book, we would appreciate your customer review on your book seller's website or on Goodreads.

Also, we would like for you to know that you can find more great books like this one at www.CreativeTexts.com